JF
Martin, Ann M.
Claudia and the first
 Thanksgiving

Other books by
Ann M. Martin

Rachel Parker, Kindergarten Show-off

Eleven Kids, One Summer

Ma and Pa Dracula

Yours Turly, Shirley

Ten Kids, No Pets

Slam Book

Just a Summer Romance

Missing Since Monday

With You and Without You

Me and Katie (the Pest)

Stage Fright

Inside Out

Bummer Summer

BABY-SITTERS LITTLE SISTER series

THE BABY-SITTERS CLUB mysteries

THE BABY-SITTERS CLUB series

CLAUDIA AND THE
FIRST THANKSGIVING

Ann M. Martin

AN
APPLE
PAPERBACK

SCHOLASTIC INC.
New York Toronto London Auckland Sydney

Cover art by Hodges Soileau

No part of this publication may be reproduced in whole or in part, or stored in a retrieval system, or transmitted in any form or by any means, electronic, mechanical, photocopying, recording, or otherwise, without written permission of the publisher. For information regarding permission, write to Scholastic Inc., 555 Broadway, New York, NY 10012.

ISBN 0-590-22875-7

12 11 10 9 8 7 6 5 4 3 2 1   5 6 7 8 9/9 0/0

Printed in the U.S.A.   40

First Scholastic printing, November 1995

The author gratefully acknowledges
Nola Thacker
for her help in
preparing this manuscript.

CLAUDIA AND THE FIRST THANKSGIVING

CHAPTER 1

"Pass the milk, please," said my older sister Janine.

"Why? Is it failing?" I asked. I cracked up.

My mother shook her head. My father made a face. Janine just looked at me.

"It's a pun," I explained.

"We know," said my mother. She smiled a little bit.

"As a humorous application of a word designed to play on two of its meanings, it was somewhat funny," said Janine. "Now, may I please have the milk?"

Okay, so maybe breakfast time is a little early for jokes. And maybe someone like me shouldn't be making jokes about passing and failing.

I picked up the milk carton and handed it to my sister.

Trust Janine to have the definition of pun right on the tip of her tongue. She is very familiar with the word "pass" as used to mean doing your schoolwork right. In fact, Janine has not only passed every course she's ever taken with triple A pluses or something, she's also taking courses at the local college, even though she's still in high school. That's because my sister, who has no sense of humor at the breakfast table, is a genuine genius.

Not me. At least, not when it comes to school. I'm much more familiar with the opposite of pass. You know, that word, fail, which means doing your schoolwork wrong. School bores me. Homework bores me. I don't understand math, and I think the rules for spelling are much too rigid. Naturally, neither my teachers nor my parents agree. My father likes math so much he works at an investment firm and my mother likes to read so much she is a librarian.

They don't understand how they could have a daughter like me.

I mean, numbers are not my thing, and neither are words (except in Nancy Drew books, which for some reason my parents don't like). I'm an artist. Colors and shapes and designs and textures — that's more like it. The world is an amazing-looking place, if you know how to look at it. And it's much more fun to describe it with images than with words.

So Janine goes on being a genius, and I work

on my art every chance I get. And someone checks my homework every night to make sure I don't fail.

"Pass the marmalade, please," I said. My sister gave it to me without comment.

There was a distressing lack of junk food on the table (I'm a junk food connoisseur) but I made up for it by stirring several spoonfuls of orange marmalade into my oatmeal. I saw Janine making a face, and I was afraid for a moment that she might launch into a lecture on Good Nutrition. Fortunately, she didn't say anything.

I could have chosen grape jelly, but it didn't fit in with my color scheme for the day. Since it was the end of October, I was wearing autumn colors: red, orange, yellow. I liked the effect I'd created. It was sort of post-modernist pumpkin.

Oh. Wait a minute. Before I describe what I look like, I guess I should say who I am.

I am Claudia Kishi. I am thirteen years old and I'm an eighth-grader at Stoneybrook Middle School in Stoneybrook, Connecticut. I have long black hair and dark brown eyes and pierced ears — one hole in my left earlobe and two holes in my right one. I live on Bradford Court, where I have lived all my life, with my mother, my father, and Janine. My grandmother, Mimi, who was my best friend, lived with us too, until she died not long ago. I still miss Mimi.

As I mentioned before, I work very hard on my art. It is, needless to say, one of the few subjects I do well in at school. I've even had my own art show, which I held in the garage. The theme was junk food images.

Besides being an artist, I am the vice-president of the Baby-sitters Club, or BSC. That's because I am one of the founding members of the club, and also because I have my own phone line in my room. But I'll tell you more about the club later.

Now, where was I? Oh. Right. My autumn fashion colors. I'd put on a pair of baggy pants, not blue, not black, but yellow. With these I was wearing my red Doc Martens, laced with orange and yellow laces, and this great, funky, enormous shirt that I found in a vintage clothes shop. It has a leaf pattern on it. The leaves are in a Hawaiian print design, and the colors are fabulous. Underneath I was wearing my red and yellow tie-dyed long underwear shirt. To complete the ensemble, I had on earrings that I'd made myself, shaped like pumpkins, and a fringed yellow-and-white scarf tied around my hair.

I looked (I modestly admit) pretty great. I did *not* look as if I belonged with the other three people sitting at the table. My mom wore a tailored navy dress with little pearl earrings. My father was wearing a navy pinstripe suit (the jacket was hanging on the back of his chair). Janine was practically a rainbow by comparison: She was dressed in a navy wool skirt and a navy v-neck sweater over a pink oxford shirt.

I finished my oatmeal. Then Mom and Dad left for work, Janine left for high school, and I grabbed my jacket (yellow, with big black buttons, also from the vintage clothes shop) and went outside to wait for my friends, so we could walk to SMS together.

Two seconds later, Stacey McGill came cruising into view. Stacey is my best friend and a fellow BSC member. She's from New York City. This is something you would know the second moment you saw her.

During the first moment you would just stare, because Stacey is off-the-scale gorgeous, with her long, blonde hair and deep blue eyes, and elegant bones. By the second moment, though, you would have taken in her cool clothes and known that she is Not From Around Here.

That's because, like me, Stacey has a style of her own. But while mine is Kishi original, hers is New York sophisticated. She was wearing an oversized midnight blue turtleneck under a cropped black wool jacket with square gold buttons. She had on black suede ankle boots, the kind that wrinkle around your ankles. Her fitted black jeans were tucked into the tops of the boots. She had looped a light blue muffler around her neck and wore matching gloves.

I waved wildly (as if we hadn't just seen each other the day before, and talked on the phone the previous night). Stacey nodded and walked over to me.

"What's happening?" she asked.

"Same old same old," I replied. "Hey, guys! Happy Halloween!" Stacey turned to see who I was talking to.

"Mar and Mal," she said with a grin.

Mary Anne Spier wrinkled her nose and Mallory Pike grinned back. They are both good friends of mine, too, as well as fellow BSC members. Mallory kept on talking as they fell into step with us.

"So I said to them, 'I don't care if you are triplets, it doesn't mean you *each* have to tell me the same duck joke.' "

Mallory lives large — at least, she lives in a large family. She is the oldest of eight siblings, three of whom are triplets. In a family that big, something outrageous is always happening, and so Mal usually has funny stories to tell. Maybe that is why she wants to be a children's book writer when she grows up.

Mary Anne, who grew up as an only child, is quiet and shy. But she is a great listener, which is probably what encouraged Mal to put such energy into the story she was telling.

"Triplet trouble?" asked Stacey.

Mal pushed her glasses up onto the bridge of her nose and answered, "No more than usual. We rented some old videos — one was a movie with the Marx Brothers called *Duck Soup* — and the triplets have been doing imitations of the comedy routines ever since."

"I love the Marx Brothers," said Stacey. "I went to a Marx Brothers movie festival once at an old theater in New York."

"I think we're about to have our own Marx Brothers festival at my house," said Mal.

"There's Logan," said Mary Anne. It was her turn to wave, very enthusiastically.

Logan Bruno is (could you have guessed?) Mary Anne's main squeeze. Mary Anne would die if she heard me describe Logan that way. But he is her boyfriend. He's a good-looking guy, a casual dresser, with blue eyes and brownish blond hair. Mary Anne thinks he looks just like the movie star Cam Geary, and I have to admit she's right. In addition to good looks, Logan has a nice Southern drawl and a way of putting you at ease that guys his age often lack. He's sensitive and understanding, too (like Mary Anne). Plus he's majorly involved in just about every sport on earth.

It's a combination that makes Logan a good baby-sitter. So Logan is in the BSC, too. He's an associate member, which means he fills in for us when we can't schedule one of our regular members for a job.

As Logan caught up to Mary Anne, she slipped her hand into his and smiled up at him. The two of them slowed down a little, so they lagged behind the rest of us as we walked. Stacey and Mal and I went into our movie reviewers mode. Since it was nearly Halloween, we concentrated heavily on the Grossest Movies Ever Made. By the time we reached Jessica Ramsey's house, we were arguing about Sickening Special Effects.

"I'm glad the triplets can't hear you," said Mal. "I don't want them getting any more disgusting ideas for their Halloween costumes." She ran around to the side door and knocked. A moment later she and Jessi were hurrying toward us. They were both giggling.

Mal and Jessi are eleven. They're in the sixth grade at SMS, and they are best friends.

Mal is medium height and sturdy and has shoulder length, reddish brown hair and a faint dusting of freckles on very pale skin. She's a jeans and sweatshirt person, which is what she was wearing today over a red checked flannel shirt. She looked as if she were ready to go horseback riding. Since Mal loves horses, it was a good look for her.

Jessi is taller and thinner, and has smooth brown skin. She loves horses, too, but she dresses more like a ballerina, which is what she wants to be someday. She often wears her dark hair pulled back into a ballerina's bun, as it was that morning. She had on a purple leotard with her jeans, and a big fuzzy lavender cardigan sweater. Not autumn colors, but definitely sensational looking.

We'd reached the hallowed halls of SMS. The usual swarm of students was hanging around outside, waiting until the last possible minute before the bell rang to go in. Even though I don't like school, I admit that I like the way SMS looks, with its weathered red brick walls and worn granite front steps. It was built before air-conditioning, which means that the windows are big, to help keep the school cool on hot days. On cold days the seats by the windows are the coldest in the classroom, but I still like to sit near them and look out, naturally.

Come to think of it, there are some other things I like about school. I don't really mind gym. Some of the other classes are okay sometimes, such as the one in which we were assigned to write our life stories. And I really like our Short Takes classes.

Short Takes is this SMS program in which all the students in all three grades take the same special class. You have the chance for six weeks at a time to study things you wouldn't ordinarily learn in school, with a different teacher in charge of each class. One of Stacey's favorite classes was called Math for Real Life. (I would call a course like that Learning to Hire an Accountant, but who asked me?) And not too long ago we had a class called Project Work, in which everyone worked three afternoons a week at a real job. Everybody in the BSC signed up for jobs at the mall, and we ended up solving a mystery there.

Today was the last day of a Short Takes unit called Learning to Read. It wasn't a class for slow readers; it was a class in how to interpret the news. Our teacher, Ms. Boyden, told us to look at stories on the same subject in different newspapers and news magazines, to see how each one of them told the story. That meant paying attention to where in the newspaper or magazine the article was placed, and even what the headlines said. (Some of the New York newspapers have really wild headlines.) We read different editorials on the same topics in different newspapers. We even looked at the advertisements, and tried to figure out who they were aimed at. That gave us clues about who the readers were, and why a newspaper or a magazine would tell a certain news story a certain way.

It was pretty amazing. For example, there was this big political march in Washington. The newspapers that supported the marchers said there were thousands and thousands of marchers. Some of the newspapers that didn't support the political cause said there were about half as many. And some of the newspapers just put a little bitty story on the back page as if there hadn't been a march at all!

"Remember that much of recent history comes from what is written in newspapers," Ms. Boyden told us. "And even history books aren't necessarily telling the truth, the whole truth, and nothing but the truth."

Pretty intense. Pretty interesting, too.

After we'd finished our last discussion in Learning to Read, a summing up of what we'd learned, Ms. Boyden grinned and held up her hands. "I've enjoyed this," she said. "Now, for your next class, you'll be doing something else that involves a different way of looking at things. A more dramatic way."

She paused. "It'll be a drama unit, and classes will be small. I'm going to read your names and the classrooms to which you are to report on Monday. Please listen carefully."

I listened *very* carefully. So far, I'd liked almost all of my Short Takes classes and this one sounded pretty promising.

"Claudia Kishi, Room two-two-six."

"Two-two-six?" I repeated.

Ms. Boyden nodded and smiled at me. I flipped open my notebook. With my purple pen, I wrote *Room 226* in big letters on my calendar for Monday.

Then I looked at the clock with a sense of deep satisfaction. It was Friday, and school was almost over for the day, and for the week. I've said it before, and I'll say it again: Friday is the best day of the whole week, starting when the last bell after the last class begins to ring!

CHAPTER 2

"Have you ever noticed how all the holidays come at once?" I complained. "And that they really stack up when the weather starts turning bad? I think the holidays should be changed to spring."

"Not a bad idea," agreed Logan. "Then I could devote more time to spring training."

I backed out from under my bed and ripped open the bag of potato chips I'd stashed there. They were more like potato chiplets, since the hiding place had been a little cramped, but they still tasted fine. I stared down into the bag. I was wondering if I could make a mosaic out of potato chips.

"Pass the chips," demanded Mallory, putting an end to my artistic trance. I handed her the bag.

The phone rang, and Logan picked it up. "Baby-sitters Club," he said. He listened for a moment, then laughed. "No, it's not a joke.

I am a baby-sitter. This is Logan. Yes. Yes. Okay. We'll call you right back."

He hung up the phone. "Betsy Sobak," he told us. "She thought it was some kind of a practical joke when she heard my voice. Her mother let her call to set up the appointment."

Betsy Sobak is an eight-year-old charge of the BSC who is infamous for her practical jokes. (After one of her practical jokes I wound up with a broken leg!) She used to spend most of her allowance on jokes from McBuzz's Mail Order, until her parents made her quit. A baby-sitting session with Kristy Thomas, in which Kristy out-joked Betsy and totally embarrassed her, cured Betsy of the worst of her practical joke habit.

I remembered my breakfast table joke that morning and wondered if Betsy would like puns.

"Haven't you ever baby-sat for Betsy?" asked Mary Anne in surprise, reaching for the appointment book.

Logan shook his head. "I guess that's why she was surprised to hear a guy's voice on the phone," he answered.

Mary Anne set Jessi up for the job. Logan called Betsy (and Mrs. Sobak) back to confirm.

Another meeting of the BSC was in progress.

The BSC meets every Monday, Wednesday,

and Friday, from five-thirty until six, in my room. Clients know they can call us then to set up appointments. We meet in my room because I am the only member of the BSC who has her own phone line, so when people call us for baby-sitters, we don't tie up anybody's family telephone with club business. We have seven full members and two associate members — and lots of work. Early on, we advertised our club, with signs in the supermarket and fliers, but we hardly ever have to do that anymore.

Like all businesses (according to Stacey, who lists running a small company as one of her ambitions for the future), we started small. One day Kristy, who is the president and founder of the BSC, was listening as her mom called one baby-sitter after another, trying to find a sitter for Kristy's little brother. That's when Kristy had her Great Idea. What if parents could call one number and reach several baby-sitters at once?

Kristy leaped into action, and the Baby-sitters Club was off and running (or sitting).

We have tons of regular clients, because we run the business well, and we are very good baby-sitters. For example, we schedule all our appointments in one central place, the record book. Mary Anne, who is the club secretary, is in charge of that. She has never, ever made a mistake. We also keep a club notebook (another Kristy idea), in which we write up every single baby-sitting job we go on. We read the notebook to keep up with the kids we sit for: who's developed allergies, who's having problems with a new sibling, who's become obsessed with dogs. It's a big help.

We also carry Kid-Kits to some of our jobs, particularly on rainy days, or when kids are sick and have to stay inside. Kid-Kits are boxes we have filled with old toys and games and books, plus stickers and markers and whatever else we think kids might like. Although most of the things are hand-me-downs, they are brand-new to the kids we sit for. Needless to say, when we show up with Kid-Kits, we are *very* welcome.

Kristy, who thought up the Kid-Kits, hurtles through life at top speed, running the BSC, coaching a softball team for little kids called Kristy's Krushers, doing her homework, and coming up with great ideas, many of them for the BSC. She is major energy in a small, plain package. Not that Kristy is plain — she isn't. She's short (the shortest person in the eighth grade) and cute, with brown hair and brown eyes. But her style is basic and no-nonsense: turtleneck, jeans, running shoes, and sometimes a baseball cap with a picture of a collie on it in memory of Louie, her old collie who died not so long ago.

Another Kristy fact: She is not shy about saying what she thinks, loudly and often. I think that's because she grew up with two older brothers, Charlie and Sam, and a younger brother, David Michael. Kristy's big brothers acted like, well, big brothers, usually teasing Kristy, sometimes letting her tag along. Kristy learned early to speak up and to stand up for herself.

When David Michael was a baby (he's seven now), Kristy's father just left one day and didn't come back. Things were tough for the Thomases for a long time after that. Then Mrs. Thomas met Watson Brewer, and they fell in love and got married. And Kristy, who'd lived all her life next door to Mary Anne and across the street from me on Bradford Court, moved with her family into Watson's house across town.

It's no ordinary house, either. Watson Brewer is a real, live millionaire, and he lives in a mansion. Now all the Thomas kids not only have rooms of their own, but they also have an even bigger family, including Watson's two kids from his first marriage, Andrew and Karen, who live with Watson every other month. Watson and Kristy's mother also recently adopted Emily Michelle, who is Vietnamese. After that, Kristy's grandmother Nannie moved in, to help take care of Emily Michelle (and everyone else). Kristy's new, bigger family also includes a Bernese mountain dog puppy named Shannon, Boo-Boo the cranky cat, a couple of goldfish, other assorted, er, wildlife, and maybe, just maybe, the ghost of Ben Brewer, one of Watson's ancestors.

You've already met Mary Anne. She's one of the founding members of the BSC, too, and she is also Kristy's best friend. If you think that shy, sensitive Mary Anne and high-energy, high-impact Kristy are very different, you are right. But maybe that's what makes them such good friends. They've known each other since they were babies. As I mentioned, they used to live next door to each other, until Kristy moved to the mansion — and Mary Anne and her dad moved into a haunted farmhouse. (Two new families, two haunted houses. See? Mary Anne and Kristy do have a lot in common.)

Before the move, Mary Anne was an only child. Her mother died when Mary Anne was just a baby, and Mr. Spier raised Mary Anne very strictly, even choosing the clothes she wore (little kid clothes, long after she wasn't a little kid anymore). As a single parent, he wanted to make sure he did everything right. I think it worked. Mary Anne is a terrific person. And when she finally convinced her father that she was growing up, and was responsible enough to choose her own clothes and have a little more freedom, her father loosened up a bit.

Right about then he started spending time with his old high school sweetheart, Sharon Schafer, who'd just moved back to Stoneybrook (from California) after getting divorced. She brought her two kids, Dawn and Jeff, with her. Dawn, who is tall, blonde, and easygoing, and Mary Anne soon became best friends, which led naturally to Dawn's joining the BSC. And when Dawn and Mary Anne discovered that Mr. Spier and Mrs. Schafer had once dated, they lost no time in seeing to it that their parents became reacquainted. The rest is history: Mr. Spier and Mrs. Schafer got married, and Mary Anne's best friend became her stepsister. They all lived in the Schafers' farmhouse.

Sadly, though, Dawn recently decided, after a long visit with her West Coast family, that she missed her brother, her father, and California too much. (Jeff had decided pretty much the same thing earlier and had moved back.) So she headed west again. She rejoined the California version of the BSC, which she and her fellow West Coast baby-sitters call the We ♥ Kids Club. She and Mary Anne talk on the phone often, and are already planning visits. But we all really miss her.

When Dawn left, Shannon Kilbourne (who wasn't at the meeting) quit being an associate member and took over Dawn's job as alternate officer. Shannon is a neighbor of Kristy's. In fact, her Bernese mountain dog, Astrid, is the mother of the Brewer-Thomases' Bernese mountain dog puppy. Shannon has curly blonde hair and high cheekbones and she is just as organized as Kristy. She goes to a private school, makes practically straight A's, and is involved in all kinds of after-school clubs and activities. So she could replace Dawn only temporarily, because she can't come to meetings regularly.

That's where Abby Stevenson came in. She's the newest member of the BSC, and Kristy and Shannon's newest neighbor. Abby has long, dark brown hair and dark brown eyes and she's a real knockout, in more ways than one. The moment she walks into a room you *feel* her personality. She's a fast talker, and she loves jokes and puns. (*She* would have liked my jokes at breakfast.) I don't think Abby is afraid of anything — not even going eyeball to eyeball with Kristy when they don't agree about something.

Abby, who's from Long Island, is a twin. She and her sister Anna moved here with their mother, who had just received a big promotion at her job in New York City. Their father died in a car accident when Abby and Anna were nine. Abby doesn't talk about that much.

Abby and Anna turned thirteen a little while ago. They've just started to prepare to become Bat Mitzvahs in the spring, which is a very important event for many Jewish thirteen-year-olds.

Anna is the quieter of the twins. She's seriously into music and schoolwork. Abby is seriously into having a good time. She's a killer soccer player, and has a killer sense of humor.

She also has asthma, and is allergic to all kinds of things. But she doesn't let it slow her down.

Her energy is part of what makes her a great baby-sitter. I don't think there's any kid on earth who could wear her out!

Stacey is our treasurer. If this had been a Monday meeting instead of a Friday one, we'd have been paying our dues to Stacey. We grumble, but we always hand the money over. Stacey is a math whiz (one of her favorite Short Takes, remember, was Math for Real Life). She is very cool and, I have to admit, more sophisticated than the rest of us. Sometimes that's a problem. In fact, Stacey recently quit the BSC for awhile, because she started spending nearly all her time with her boyfriend Robert and his friends. Stace started missing jobs, and making lame excuses, and then she and Kristy had a big blowup. For awhile, I was the only one in the BSC who would talk to her — or whom she would talk to.

But Stacey finally realized that saying you're cool and acting cool isn't the same as being cool, which is a problem that Robert's friends had. We all started talking again and now Stacey is back handling BSC jobs and doing our numbers.

She still sees Robert, and some of his friends, sometimes. But she seems to have found a way to balance things better.

Another thing that makes Stacey seem older than the rest of us is that she has diabetes, a disease that prevents her body from managing sugar properly. That means no sweets for Stacey. It also means that she has to follow a special diet and give herself insulin shots (ewww, ow) every day. She says the shots sound worse than they are, but she does miss the sweets. As a junk food fanatic, I'm totally amazed at how much willpower Stacey has. I always make sure to keep things such as pretzels and wheat crackers and Frookies (sugarless cookies) around for our meetings, so Stacey can munch with the rest of us.

Mallory and Jessi are our junior officers. In fact, we used to baby-sit for Mallory and her brothers and sisters. Then we realized that we needed more baby-sitters, and that Mallory, thanks to all her experience with her siblings, would be an excellent BSC member. When Jessi moved to Stoneybrook and she and Mal became friends, Jessi joined the BSC, too.

You already know that Mal has seven younger brothers and sisters, including triplets: Adam, Byron, and Jordan. The other Pike siblings are Vanessa, Nicky, Margo, and Claire.

Jessi comes from a smaller family. She has a little sister named Becca and a baby brother named John Philip Ramsey, Jr., whom everybody calls Squirt. Her aunt also lives with the family, since Jessi's mother started working again.

As I mentioned, Logan is an associate member of the BSC (like Shannon is once again), and he doesn't usually come to meetings. But that afternoon, his football practice had been canceled. Now he and Abby were arguing about the merits of football versus soccer. Mary Anne was listening and rolling her eyes.

After the call from Betsy Sobak, we took three phone calls in a row. Things were pretty busy for awhile. When they'd settled down, Mary Anne said, "At least we don't have any baby-sitting jobs scheduled for Halloween."

"Good," said Stacey. "I like answering the door and seeing the costumes the little kids are wearing."

Mal grinned. "If you want to see something really scary, I'll try to bring the Pike family by your house. The triplets are all going to dress as Groucho Marx, and I think everyone else is, too."

"Seven Groucho Marxes," said Jessi. "Awesome."

We snickered at the idea.

"Speaking of baby-sitting jobs," said Kristy, "who's going to be here over Thanksgiving, and who wants to work if any jobs come up?"

"Count me out," said Abby. "We're going back to Long Island to visit all the people we left behind."

"New York City, here we come," said Mal. She crossed her fingers. "Mom's cousins have come through big time. We're going to stay in the apartment of some friends of theirs who are going to be away, and it looks like we'll have grandstand seats for the Macy's parade, too."

"New York City for me, too," Stacey put in. "I'm going to spend the whole vacation with my dad."

Jessi said, "We're going to New Jersey for Thanksgiving, but we'll be back on Saturday.

So if anything comes up over the weekend, I might be able to do it."

"My grandmother is coming from Iowa," said Mary Anne, "so I'll be here, but busy. Are the Millers still coming to visit you, Kristy?"

"Yup," said Kristy, looking pleased. Her Aunt Colleen and Uncle Wallace are some of her favorite relatives. Plus they'd be bringing their four kids, who are also favorites of Kristy's.

"Here, but *very* busy," Mary Anne murmured, making a note of it in her record book.

"I'll be here," I said. "But not quite so busy, I guess. My aunt and uncle are coming to dinner, too." My Aunt Peaches and Uncle Russ, who live in Stoneybrook, are *my* favorite aunt and uncle. Especially my aunt. She is major fun. I was really looking forward to spending Thanksgiving with her and Russ.

"We're going to my cousins', in Louisville," reported Logan.

"And Shannon and her family are going to a bed-and-breakfast inn to ski in Vermont," added Mary Anne, making one last note.

"It's going to be a great Thanksgiving," I burst out. "It's my favorite, favorite holiday."

Stacey smiled. "Even though you don't get presents on Thanksgiving, the way you do at Christmas?"

"Maybe that's why I like it so much," I said, more thoughtfully. "You don't have to worry about buying presents or making them, or wrapping them — not that I don't love all that stuff, too. You just hang out with your favorite people and eat all your favorite foods: pumpkin pie, candied sweet potatoes . . ."

"Sweet potato pie," added Logan, "and pecan pie."

"Hey, don't forget the turkey," said Kristy. "And the dressing and the . . ."

We were off and running. Then suddenly it was six and the meeting was over.

We'd finished the gourmet junk food I'd provided, too. Even the pretzels.

All that talk about Thanksgiving dinner must have made us extra hungry.

I grinned as I waved good-bye to everybody. It was a good thing Halloween was coming. I could buy plenty of candy at half price the day after — more than enough to last until Turkey Day!

CHAPTER 3

Over the weekend Stacey and I had discovered that we were both assigned to Room 226 for our next Short Takes class. We'd spent a good bit of time since then speculating on who our teacher would be. So far, neither of us had had the same teacher twice.

When I arrived in Room 226 on Monday, I immediately looked to see who our teacher was — and relaxed. It was Ms. Garcia. I'd never had her before, but I'd heard she was decent.

"Hi," I said. "I'm Claudia."

Ms. Garcia, who was leaning against the edge of her desk, nodded. "Hi, Claudia. Take a seat anywhere. We'll get started as soon as the bell rings."

I slid in behind Stacey. A moment later, just as the bell had finished ringing, Abby burst through the door and hurled herself into a desk in the front of the room.

I hid a smile. It was a classic Abby entrance, and very dramatic. She would probably do well in our Drama Short Takes class.

Ms. Garcia introduced herself, and we went around the room saying our names. The class wasn't big, only fifteen students.

"This segment of Short Takes will be structured slightly differently from the others. Each Short Takes class will work on a different drama project. One class will perform a play at SMS, one will study plays as literature, one will study playwrights, and so forth. Our class will venture into drama for children: We will write a play for the third-graders at SES, then follow the project through to an actual performance by the children in front of an audience."

"I like this, I think," I whispered to Stacey.

In the front, Abby's hand shot up.

"Yes?" said Ms. Garcia.

"We choose the topic, we write the play, we cast it, we stage it? The whole bit?"

"The whole bit," Ms. Garcia agreed, looking amused.

"Well, then, hadn't we better get started? I mean, we don't have much time."

I cracked up. Ms. Garcia didn't seem to mind, though. "You're right," she told Abby. "Why don't we begin with a discussion group, to decide on the topic for the play?"

"We could do a circus," I suggested. "Eight-year-olds love circuses." We'd had a summer circus camp for some of the kids we baby-sit for and it had been a huge success.

"A circus is a good idea," said Ms. Garcia, writing it down on her notepad.

"Soccer," said Abby. She was immediately seconded by Rick Chow. I used to sit with Rick and some of his friends at lunch, before the BSC started eating together.

"I don't know anything about soccer," Erica Blumberg objected.

"A sports theme is a good idea, Abby," said Ms. Garcia, "but — "

"Hey, you don't have to wrap it up in cotton candy for me," said Abby. "It won't kill me if we don't do a third-grade play about soccer." She grinned at Erica. Erica looked a little confused, but she gave Abby a smile back.

Suggestions flew around the room, not only for themes, but for plot ideas, too. For awhile we toyed with the idea of a fairy tale, maybe even making it a funny, slapstick one. The circus idea was discussed a lot, too.

My mind drifted. I started thinking about pumpkin pie. Pecan pie. Thanksgiving . . .

"Thanksgiving!" I suddenly blurted out.

"Don't worry, you didn't miss it, Claud," Abby joked. "November's just starting."

"No! Why not have Thanksgiving as the

29

theme of the play? I mean, who doesn't like Thanksgiving?" I, of course, was thinking of Thanksgiving dinner.

"Third-graders would probably love that," said Erica. "And it has a built-in plot. I mean, you know, the first Thanksgiving and all."

"True. But, there's more to Thanksgiving than the feast," said Ms. Garcia. "If someone were to go back to the real first Thanksgiving he or she might be in for quite a surprise. It was, I imagine, quite different from the way we celebrate Thanksgiving now."

"Yeah," Abby said. "Like the roles of men and women. Those have changed."

"And the relationship between European settlers and Indians," added Rick Chow.

"Indians," repeated Abby, aghast. "You mean 'Native Americans.' "

"But 'Native American' could refer to anyone who was born in America," said Erica. "*I* could be a Native American."

"What about 'First American'?" I suggested. "I've heard that term."

"How about using the name of the people? You know, like Iroquois or Wampanoag?" said Abby.

"That's fine if you know the name," replied Ms. Garcia. She thought for a moment. Finally she said, "For the sake of our discussions, and also for the sake of the play, why don't we stick to 'Native American' or to the name of the people, okay?"

"Okay," my classmates and I murmured.

We returned to the subject of the first Thanksgiving.

"I bet the menu has changed some, too," I said.

Stacey said, "So why don't we tell it like it really was? Why don't we have someone go back to the real first Thanksgiving? Sort of a time traveler, who could point out some of the differences to the audience."

"Like a Greek chorus," said Erica, nodding wisely.

That confused most of the kids in the room until Ms. Garcia said, "A good point, Erica. In Greek drama, long ago, a chorus stood to one side of the action and sang about, or commented on, everything that was happening onstage."

"So what now?" asked Abby. "We have a ton of research to do, right? At the library and all that?"

I groaned.

I wasn't the only one.

Ms. Garcia nodded. "If we're all agreed on Thanksgiving as a theme, I'd say that's the next step. Everybody needs to gather the facts about the first Thanksgiving. A good place to begin is with children's books, for basic information."

"Children's books? Like *picture* books?" I asked.

"Exactly like that, Claudia," Ms. Garcia said.

Not bad, I decided. I could definitely handle picture books. Several artists I admired had illustrated picture books. And who knows? Maybe there was a Nancy Drew book about Thanksgiving that I had somehow overlooked.

"The real Thanksgiving?" Jessi tilted her head thoughtfully. "Interesting, Claud."

"Yes," I said. We were halfway through our Monday BSC meeting, later that day. We'd handed our dues over to Stacey, who was balancing our accounts. Mal was writing in the club notebook and smiling to herself. Kristy had folded her arms, and was surveying her kingdom. Mary Anne was flipping through the record book. Abby and Jessi were doing some kind of stretching exercise that was "good for tight hamstrings." They had been comparing notes on various muscle stretches required for sports and ballet. I was going through all the pockets of all the coats in my closet, looking for a bag of candy corn that I *knew* I had hidden there only a few days earlier. Did we have mice? Had they found it and carried it away? Should I start looking for a trail of candy corn leading to their hideout?

"Well, there is one difference between Thanksgiving then and now," said Jessi.

"What difference is that?" I asked, not really paying attention. Maybe it hadn't been a coat pocket. Maybe it had been one of my old purses.

"No African Americans were at the first Thanksgiving," said Jessi.

I backed out of the closet and gave Jessi a surprised look. "Well, of course they weren't. These were English guys. I don't think there were all that many Africans living in England at the time. Or Asians, either."

"There were Jews, though," said Abby suddenly. "But not at the first Thanksgiving."

"That's a good point," said Stacey. "It's one of the things we should try to bring up in the play. I mean, isn't that our theme? Thanksgiving then and now, the truth and the, the . . ."

"Fictional trimmings," said Mal suddenly.

"Good luck," said Jessi. She grinned. "And I thought we had a tough subject for *our* Drama Short Takes!"

"What's yours?" asked Kristy.

"World Drama," Jessi replied. "We're supposed to look at plays from several different countries, and study how they are alike and how they are different, in their subject matter and their staging."

Mal said contentedly, "We're doing Drama as Literature. I'm not quite sure what that means yet. But it's going to involve a lot of reading."

"Kristy and I are in the same class," said Mary Anne. "It's called Books, Plays, and Movies. We're going to look at books that have been turned into plays and movies. Like *The Incredible Journey*. It's been made into two movies by Walt Disney, you know. One is called *The Incredible Journey*, and one is called *Homeward Bound*."

"Do you get to vid in class?" asked Jessi. "Lucky you!"

Just then the phone started ringing. We scheduled some appointments, including one for Kristy over the Thanksgiving holidays.

"I thought your aunt and uncle and all their kids were coming," Abby said.

"Nope." Kristy shook her head and made a face. "Uncle Neal broke his leg, so Aunt Colleen and Uncle Wallace are going up to help him and Aunt Theo for the holidays. Uncle Neal's invited a whole bunch of his relatives." Aunt Theo is the middle sister in Kristy's mother's family. She's married to Neal Meiner, a guy who likes to smoke cigars and talk loudly. He is not Kristy's favorite relative.

"That's too bad," I said.

Kristy shrugged. "We'll still have a ton of

people," she said. But I could tell she was disappointed.

"Aha!" I shrieked, holding up a bulging sock.

Everyone jumped.

"The candy corn," I explained. "I *knew* I'd hidden it in something like a pocket."

For a moment everyone looked blank. Then Kristy checked her watch and quickly cleared her throat. "This meeting of the Baby-sitters Club," she said, "is hereby adjourned!"

CHAPTER 4

"I think this *lunch* is from the first Thanksgiving," said Kristy. She eyed her lunch tray disapprovingly.

"I'm pretty sure green Jell-O wasn't on the menu," said Stacey.

"No, but I think it was on the *Mayflower*," cracked Abby. "As glue to hold the ship together."

We all groaned.

It had been a busy week. Halloween had come and gone. Mal and her father had escorted seven Groucho Marxes on a trick-or-treat expedition. We had been serenaded at our house by a trio of singing pumpkins led by Karen Brewer, Kristy's seven-year-old stepsister, while Kristy and her sort-of boyfriend Bart Taylor hovered in the background. Squirt had been frightened by a kid in a ghost costume when he'd answered the door with Jessi. We'd all been working on our Short Takes projects. And we'd had a very busy baby-sitting week. So busy, in fact, that I'd taken a job that had lasted right through our Wednesday afternoon meeting.

Missing a meeting is on Kristy's list of "The Top Ten Worst Things a Baby-sitter Can Do." Sickness (like Mal's mononucleosis) or major emergencies were about the only acceptable reasons, and any day now I expected Kristy to start asking for doctor's notes if we didn't come because we were sick.

The only other approved reason to miss a meeting, of course, was a baby-sitting job.

So I didn't quake when Kristy turned her attention from her green Jello-O to me and asked, "How was it yesterday?" Her tone was mild and unaccusing. She meant, how did the baby-sitting job go?

"It went fine," I said. "The twins were still a little wired from Halloween. Mrs. Arnold had really thrown herself into it, and the decorations were still up. Plus she'd made trays and trays of Halloween cupcakes."

"Poor Claudia." Stacey clasped her hands together in mock sympathy. "Were you forced to eat cupcakes?"

I stuck my nose in the air. "I'll have you know that I'm a responsible baby-sitter. Marilyn and Carolyn and I only had one cupcake each, with milk, in the middle of the afternoon. I didn't want them to spoil their dinner."

I paused, then added, "But Mrs. Arnold did give me some extra cupcakes to take home."

Mary Anne sat down at the table. Her eyes were red, as if she had been crying.

"Mary Anne, what's wrong?" I asked.

She looked surprised. "Nothing," she answered. Then she said to Kristy, "And don't you dare say anything about how gross lunch looks today, either."

"She already did," I said. "She said she thought it was leftovers from the first Thanksgiving. Then Abby said . . ."

"I don't want to know," said Mary Anne, putting her hands over her ears.

She waited a minute to make sure we really had stopped talking about the latest lunchroom loser plate and then lowered her hands. "Speaking of Thanksgiving," she said, "my grandmother can't make it."

"That's too bad," said Stacey.

"I know. I haven't seen her since I went to visit her after my grandfather died."

Mary Anne's maternal grandparents, who lived on a farm in Iowa, had raised her from when her mother died until she was eighteen months old. There had been a custody dispute when her father had wanted her back. But it had been settled without too much of a fuss (I think). Mary Anne's last visit to her grandmother had been a big success, and she'd been looking forward to seeing her grandmother again, especially since Dawn wasn't going to be around for Thanksgiving.

"Bad news," said Kristy sympathetically.

Mary Anne said, "The worst. She can't get a nonstop flight. The only flight available had a million-hour layover in Atlanta. Can you believe it?"

"Poor Mary Anne," I said. "Is that why you were crying?"

"Crying? I wasn't — " Mary Anne stopped, then burst out laughing. "No, that's not why I was crying."

"You *were* crying?" asked Stacey.

"No! Yes. I mean, I was crying, but it was in my Short Takes class. We started watching *The Incredible Journey*. Two dogs and a cat try to find their way home through the wilderness. It's sooo sad." Mary Anne started sounding a little choked up.

"It's a cool movie," said Abby unexpectedly. "Don't worry. It has a happy ending. I give it four barks."

"Woof, woof," said Kristy. "Woof, woof."

"Meow, meow, meow, meow," chimed in Stacey.

The teary look left Mary Anne's face. We all started to laugh.

"Hey, Claudia," said Jessi.

I turned, holding my locker open.

"I'm glad I finally found you. I was about to stash these in my locker and give up," Jessi said. She fished around in her backpack and pulled out a couple of paperback picture books. "These are Becca's," she said. "She's mostly outgrown them now, but they might help you with your Thanksgiving project."

She handed the books to me. The one on top had a photograph of a young girl in what looked like Pilgrim clothing. The title was *Sarah Morton's Day*.

"Thanks," I said. I put the books in my locker, pulled out my math notebook (ugh), and turned around to walk with Jessi. "Did you hear that Mary Anne's grandmother isn't coming for Thanksgiving?"

"Yup. And we're not going to New Jersey, either," Jessi said.

"You're kidding! Why not?"

"You're not going to believe this. My relatives in Oakley were invited along on a church retreat. They'd been on the waiting list, and some spaces opened up. So that's that. We'll be in Stoneybrook for Thanksgiving."

"That won't be so bad, will it?" I asked.

"No," said Jessi, stopping outside her classroom. "I wanted to see everybody, of course, but I guess it can wait. See you later."

"See ya," I said. Wow, I thought, as I went to my math class. Kristy, Mary Anne, and Jessi had all had their T-day plans canceled. I sure hoped it wasn't contagious. I really wanted to spend Thanksgiving with Peaches.

"I'm sorry, Claudia," said my aunt's voice on the phone Sunday night. "You know we wanted to spend Thanksgiving with you. Russ didn't even know he had any relatives left in Ireland. So when they called and said they were going to be in the United States, how could we not invite them for Thanksgiving? They won't arrive until Thanksgiving morning, and we have to go to meet the train from New York. They'll be all jet-lagged. We're just going to stay here and have a quiet dinner. You can meet them later on when they've settled in."

I was silent. I didn't want my favorite aunt to feel bad. But I felt pretty bad myself. Finally I said, "I'll look forward to meeting them."

"Good." My aunt sounded relieved. "And we'll do something special together soon. Maybe a trip to the monkey bars in the park."

I laughed, feeling a little better. When I was a kid, my amazing Aunt Peaches would take me to the park. She'd swing on the swings, slide down the slides, and hang from the monkey bars with me. It was one of the many reasons she was my favorite relative.

"Guess what?" I said as we stood on the steps that Monday morning, waiting for the first bell to ring.

"Your aunt and uncle can't come for Thanksgiving," guessed Stacey. Her mother had given her a ride to school, and she'd just joined me, Mary Anne, Jessi, Mal, Abby, and Kristy (whose bus, for once, had been early).

My mouth dropped open. My aunt and uncle had called with their bad news the night before, too late for me to call Stacey and tell her. "How did you know?"

Stacey said, "Really? Truly? I just guessed."

"Yup. Russ has long-lost relatives from Ireland who are showing up Thanksgiving Day."

"Wow," said Abby. She cleared her throat. "Actually, we're not going to Long Island, either. My mom has a major project she has to work on. She'll be lucky if she can manage to take Thanksgiving Day off."

Stacey started to snicker.

We all looked at her in surprise.

"I'm sorry," said Stacey. "It's just that, well, I'm not going to New York for Thanksgiving, either. My mom and dad got things totally mixed up. He's actually going to be out of town, so it'll be Mom and me in good old Stoneybrook. I mean, can you believe it? This is the Thanksgiving of Doom for the BSC. Every single one of us has had our plans fall through except Mal."

We looked at Mal expectantly.

"No way," said Mal. "We're absolutely, positively going to New York. Trust me."

Kristy had just called our Monday afternoon BSC meeting to order.

Mal said, "Pass the turkey."

"What do you mean? I have candy corn, and leftover chocolate candy in pumpkin wrappers, but no turkey," I told her.

Mal shook her head and looked around at the rest of us.

"Or maybe I should ask for crow," she said. "Isn't that what you eat when you're wrong about something?"

Stacey caught on first. "Oh, no, Mal. Not New York!"

"Not New York is right," answered Mal. "We're not going to New York. Marie and Phil called. The apartment we were going to stay in is totally under water. A pipe in the apartment above it broke. They're just hoping they can have it cleaned up in time for Christmas."

"What about hotels?" asked Kristy.

"Booked solid, at least the ones we could afford. We talked about driving in just to see the parade, but Mom and Dad said the traffic would be too bad."

"The traffic would be evil," declared Stacey. "I'm really sorry, Mal. I wish there was something we could do. I would ask my dad if you could use his apartment, but he's having the carpets cleaned while he's away. It's only a one-bedroom, anyway. . . ."

Her voice trailed off. We sat silently for a moment, contemplating Thanksgiving celebrations that weren't meant to be.

Kristy frowned thoughtfully. "Hmm," she murmured.

"So it'll be a Pike family Thanksgiving in Stoneybrook," said Jessi.

"Yeah. Maybe my brothers and sisters will put on a parade," said Mal glumly.

"Hmmmm," said Kristy again. "If you counted everyone in everyone's family who is in the BSC, how many people would that be?"

Stacey did some quick calculations in her head (while I was still trying to figure out the question) and said, "Thirty-five, no, thirty-six people — not including Shannon and her family, or Logan and his family."

"No. No, I'm not counting them," said Kristy.

Mary Anne's expression of sympathy for

Mal turned to one of indignation.

"What I mean is, not for this. What if we, well, wouldn't it be fun if we could have Thanksgiving together? All of our families?"

"Great idea!" I burst out.

"Super," said Jessi.

"It *would* be fun," said Mal, looking slightly more cheerful.

"Thirty-six people?" repeated Mary Anne. She sounded stunned.

Stacey grabbed a piece of paper and began to write out a list. "Yup, thirty-six," she said after a minute. "Squirt would be the youngest. Nannie would be the oldest."

"Awesome," I said. "How could we do it?"

"A restaurant, maybe," Abby said. "You know, rent a banquet room. That would probably be expensive, though."

"It would be less expensive if we cooked dinner ourselves. But cooking for a lot of people is a lot of work," said Mal. She definitely knew what she was talking about.

The phone rang. "Let's think about it," said Kristy. "We'll brainstorm. We'll come up with something. This is clearly a job for . . ." She picked up the phone, grinned at us, and said briskly, "The Baby-sitters Club."

CHAPTER 5

Doing research on Thanksgiving meant going to the library. If you think having a mother who is the head librarian is an advantage when it comes to fact-hunting, you're right.

But it's not as big an advantage as you might think. You still have to look up everything yourself. Actually, the main advantage is that the head librarian gives you a ride home afterward.

On Tuesday, Stacey and Abby and I headed for the library, specifically, the children's section, where we'd decided to do a lot of our research. SMS isn't far from the library, so we walked there after school.

"Hello, Claudia," said my mom. I'd told her we were coming. She'd promised us a ride home if we were still there when she quit work for the day.

Behind the front desk with my mom, holding a notebook in his hand, was a student librarian. You know, like a student teacher. "Donald, this is my younger daughter Claudia, and her friends Stacey and Abby," my mom said.

We all said hello. And Donald added, "I know your sister Janine. She's in one of my classes at college."

"Great," I replied. I mean, what can you say to a comment like that?

Abby said, "We're here to do research for our Short Takes class at school. On Thanksgiving."

"That's a big subject," said my mom. "Could you narrow it down for us?"

Quickly we explained our drama project. "So we think we should do most of our research in the kids' section. You know, to keep it easy enough for the third-graders to understand," Abby concluded.

"I'm sure you know how to use the computer catalog to look up subjects and find out where the books are," Donald said to me.

"Ah, well," I mumbled.

"I do," said Stacey. "Are the children's books cataloged with the adult books in the computer?"

Donald nodded. "The children's books, both fiction and nonfiction, are listed with the letter 'J' in front of the call number. That means juvenile books. A JP means juvenile picture book. JE means juvenile easy reader."

"Thanks," said Abby.

"You know where the children's books are?" Donald asked.

I could give Donald a more enthusiastic yes on that. I might not be a big reader, but some of my earliest memories involve coming to the library with my mom or with Mimi, and sitting in the cheerfully decorated children's room, looking at JPs while Janine loaded up with books for (much) older readers. And I had very definite tastes in picture book illustrators even before I could read. So when I'd come to visit my mom at her new job at this library, the first place I'd checked out was the children's room.

Stacey scanned through the computer and we made a list of possibilities. Then we headed for the children's room. It was practically empty. We divided up the titles and went in search of them, then regrouped at a table in a corner.

"Whew," said Abby, thumping down an armload of books. "Thanksgiving is a very popular topic."

"Some of these books are ancient," I said. "Look at this one. The pages are starting to turn yellow."

Abby and I settled in and started taking notes. Stacey had headed off for the adult reference section, to see if she could find any books about the Pilgrims and the first Thanksgiving there. After awhile I realized that she hadn't returned.

"I wonder where Stacey is," I said.

"Beats me," said Abby, flipping the pages of a book called *Molly's Pilgrim*. "Check this out, Claudia. It says that the Pilgrims' idea for celebrating Thanksgiving came from the Jewish holiday of Tabernacles. It's what we call Sukkot now."

"Really?" I said. "Let me see that when you're through."

"Sure."

I stood up and went to look for Stacey. She was standing in the stacks reading. The title of the book was *Good Money.*

"Um, Stacey?"

She slammed the book shut guiltily. "It's about how to invest money in good things. You know, companies that don't hurt the environment," she explained.

"So check it out and take it home," I said, using the stern librarian tone I'd heard my mother use. "Right now the subject is Pilgrims. And Thanksgiving."

By the time the library closed, we had pages and pages of notes, and about half a dozen books we'd checked out. That's the other main advantage of having a mother who's the head librarian. You can wait until the library is almost closed and still check your books out.

Other people in our class had been doing research, too, of course. Erica had even gone to the college library. Our class spent the rest of the week putting our notes together and passing around the books we'd gathered. Then we made up a story. We kept it pretty simple.

In the story, it is the night before Thanksgiving. A girl named Alice falls asleep. (We chose Alice because of *Alice in Wonderland*.) She wakes up at the first Thanksgiving. No one can see her except for the Pilgrim and Native American children. As they help prepare the feast, the children and Alice talk.

Alice learns about their Thanksgiving, and tells them about Thanksgiving now. She is as amazed by some of their customs and foods as they are by her stories of the present. Alice doesn't quite believe them about *everything*. And they don't quite believe Alice.

From time to time Alice turns to the audience to act as a narrator, and to make comments about the differences between the first Thanksgiving and the holiday we celebrate today. She talks about the different roles of women then and now (and how women still aren't treated as equals), the relationship between the Native Americans and the Pilgrims and how that has also changed. Alice points out the fact that although the Pilgrims came to the "New World" for religious freedom, they didn't always tolerate the religions of others, or encourage independent thinking, for that matter. It wasn't very long after the first Thanksgiving that women — and a few men — were hanged as witches in Salem, Massachusetts.

When the feast is ready, the children hurry to join in. Alice turns to the audience and says there is much to celebrate now, as there was then, but there is still much work to be done. Thanksgiving is a celebration of what has been done, and what can be done. Then she yawns . . . and wakes up, back in the present, as her mother calls her to start getting ready for Thanksgiving.

We officially presented the final copy of the script to Ms. Garcia the following Monday.

Ms. Garcia really liked it. "I'm very impressed," she said. "You have been thorough, accurate, and original, yet the play is simple enough to appeal to any third-grader. I'll make copies. I'm going to assign costume and set design planning for tonight's homework. We'll discuss that tomorrow, and then on Wednesday, we'll go to Stoneybrook Elementary School to meet our third-graders."

I was assigned to scenery design, Pilgrim

division. That evening, I settled down with a pile of picture books from the library. I had just started sketching a Pilgrim house when the phone rang.

"Claudia. Good. You're home."

"Hi, Kristy," I said.

"Listen, you know Thanksgiving?"

"More than you would ever believe," I answered, looking at the stack of picture books.

That blew right by Kristy. She was focused on an idea, and nothing was going to stop her. "You know how everyone's plans fell through, and we've been trying to figure out how we could all have Thanksgiving together?"

"Thirty-six people," I said. "The Pilgrims had ninety Native Americans, plus their chief, at the first Thanksgiving."

"Well, we don't have that many," said Kristy, unimpressed. "But I was thinking: Why not have Thanksgiving dinner at my house? I mean, it's big enough."

"Kristy!" I gasped. "That's a super idea. And much nicer than a restaurant or a hotel banquet room."

"I thought so," Kristy said, sounding very satisfied with herself. Then she paused, "Of course, I don't know what my mother and Watson will think of the idea."

"If anybody can convince them, you can,"

I said. It was true. Kristy is the definition of determined. I sometimes think that people do what she wants because it's easier than trying to oppose her.

"Why don't we talk about it at our next meeting," I suggested. "We can plan how you'll present the idea of a mega-Thanksgiving feast to them."

"Okay. Great. Will you call Stacey and let her know? I'll call Mary Anne, and she can phone Abby, and — "

"And Stacey can tell Jessi, and Jessi can phone Mal," I finished.

"Done," said Kristy. "See you tomorrow."

She hung up the phone. Kristy doesn't waste time — or words.

"Pumpkin pie, pecan pie, sweet potato pie," I hummed, as I went back to designing Pilgrim scenery.

CHAPTER 6

"Do you think you can stay together, or should I assign you partners?" asked Ms. Garcia, her eyes twinkling. We all groaned.

"Come on, then. Let's go."

It was Wednesday. Our Short Takes class headed out the door of SMS and over to Stoneybrook Elementary School, to meet the prospective cast and crew of *Alice and the Pilgrims.*

The third-graders had assembled in the auditorium. I admit, I was a little daunted when we walked through the door and all those eager faces turned toward us. Plus the energy generated by that many third-graders in one place is amazing. Naturally, we three BSC members saw some faces in the crowd we recognized, such as Becca Ramsey and Charlotte Johanssen.

The principal, Ms. Reynolds, took it in stride. She welcomed us and motioned us onto the stage, where we sat in a row of chairs. She followed us onto the stage, then held up her hands and cleared her throat.

"Can everybody hear me?" Ms. Reynolds asked. Her voice wasn't very loud, but it was penetrating. I watched in amazement as three classes of third-graders settled down.

Ms. Reynolds introduced our class. Then we went down the row and said our names. Erica explained our drama project and told the kids that we had written a play about Thanksgiving for them.

Then it was Abby's turn. She explained that we needed actors, director's assistants, and a stage crew. "We're giving your teachers a sign-up sheet to post in your classrooms. We're also going to give each teacher a list of the characters in the play, plus a list of the different kinds of jobs you can do if you don't want to be onstage. You can sign up to try out for a part in the play, or help paint scenery, make costumes, or be an assistant. On Friday, after school, we're going to hold tryouts for parts in the play. Next week, after school each day and all next weekend, we'll rehearse and make the costumes and scenery. We'll put on the play the Monday before Thanksgiving, and you can invite your families, friends, and teachers to come."

Excited murmurs were building in the auditorium. Ms. Reynolds stepped in again, and calmed the kids down enough for them to be led back to their classrooms.

"It looks as if you are going to have a lot of eager volunteers," she said, turning and smiling at us.

"We hope so," said Abby. "We've written a great play."

"I'm sure you have," said Ms. Reynolds. "See you Friday afternoon."

Did I say that the auditorium full of third-graders was noisy on Wednesday?

Wednesday was *peaceful* compared to Friday afternoon. The sign-up sheets were a jumble of names, half in careful letters, half almost unreadable. And the auditorium itself was a jumble of the kids at high speed. Fortunately, the principal and one of the third grade teachers had stayed after school to help out, so with Ms. Garcia and the fifteen of us in the Short Takes class, we had enough people to hold the auditions.

Barely.

I recognized many of the names from baby-sitting. Becca Ramsey and Charlotte Johanssen had signed up for costumes and scenery. That figured. Charlotte had overcome enough of her shyness to be a cheerleader for Kristy's softball team, the Krushers, but she still hates the idea of being onstage. And although Becca loves to try to imitate Jessi's ballet moves, she's not crazy about any kind of performance.

I was glad to see that they had decided to participate anyway.

The kids who were trying out for parts, by and large, didn't have any problems with shyness. Nicky Pike and Buddy Barrett both wanted to play Native Americans. But not just any Native Americans — they wanted to be chiefs.

"With big feather headdresses," stated Nicky firmly.

"Not possible," said Rick Chow, looking frazzled.

Nicky crossed his arms and frowned ferociously. "Why not?"

"We'll explain later," said Rick. "Go stand over there with the others who want to play Native Americans."

"Miles Standishes, Giles Hopkinses, and Remember Allertons over here!" I heard Abby shout.

Meanwhile, the rest of us were rounding up students and handing out copies of the lines we wanted them to read. We decided not to hand out the scripts until after we'd cast the play.

"I want to be Miles Standish," announced Carolyn Arnold.

"Ha!" Jake Kuhn scoffed. "You can't be. You're a girl, not a boy!"

"Well, then, you can't be Squanto," Carolyn shot back, "because you're not really a Native American!"

That stopped Jake for a moment. I hastily intervened. "Of course you can try out for the part of Miles Standish, Carolyn. That's what acting is all about — pretending to be a different person."

Jake frowned, but he didn't say anything else. Carolyn gave him a triumphant look and went over to join the "Miles Standishes."

At last everyone was organized, and the tryouts began. The kids read their lines in pairs.

"Welcome to this land," Buddy Barrett shouted. "Welcome to our home."

"We have traveled far across the water to find a new home and freedom," Marilyn Arnold shouted back.

"Whoa, whoa, whoa!" called Abby, her hands over her ears. "Why are you shouting?"

"So everyone can hear us?" said Buddy.

"You don't have to shout," Abby explained. "Talk in a loud, clear voice. But *don't shout*."

58

"You're shouting," said Marilyn.

Abby wrinkled her nose. "Let's cut a deal, okay? I don't shout, you don't shout. Deal?"

"Deal," said Marilyn. She turned to Buddy.

"We have traveled *far* across the water," she repeated. "But how do you know our language?"

Jake folded his arms and looked smug. "I've been around," he said.

Everyone cracked up. We had to start over again.

We really weren't looking for Academy Award actors. We just wanted to make sure the kids were comfortable on the stage and could be heard. We'd pretty much decided to give roles to everybody who tried out, though they wouldn't necessarily be cast in the roles they'd tried out for.

Betsy Sobak's acting came as a nice surprise. Although she'd looked at the sheet of paper with her lines for only a few minutes, she spoke in a clear, carrying voice without reading. She paused and turned and even gestured.

It was awesome.

"Don't look now," I whispered to Stacey, "but I think we just found our Alice."

When we had finished reading, we thanked everybody for coming. The principal reminded the kids that rehearsals would begin on Monday after school. "We'll post the list of parts, so you can find out first thing Monday morning," she told the third-graders. "And we'll give out copies of the script then, too."

After the kids had left, we were able to cast the play pretty quickly. There weren't many major roles. Betsy Sobak won the role of Alice by unanimous consent. We argued a little over letting Carolyn Arnold be Miles Standish, but eventually we decided to do that. Some of the girls were going to have to be Pilgrim men, anyway, since by the end of the first winter, only six of the eighteen married women who sailed aboard the *Mayflower* were left alive in the colony.

None of the boys had tried out for Pilgrim women roles. Hmmm . . .

In the end, everyone who didn't get a speaking part was cast as a Pilgrim or a Native American. Besides Alice, the main characters were: two Pilgrim children, a girl and a boy, to be played by Marilyn Arnold and Buddy Barrett; Squanto, the sole survivor of the Pautuxet people, who'd acted as an interpreter for the Pilgrims and the Wampanoag people, to be played by Jake Kuhn; and Massasoit, the Chief of the Wampanoag people, to be played by James Hobart.

We handed the list over to the principal and headed out of the auditorium.

"We're making good progress," said Abby.

Stacey looked at her watch. "We better make even better progress right now. Our BSC meeting starts in twelve minutes."

I shrieked, "Oh, no! The Kristy monster!"

We began to run for my house.

CHAPTER 7

Monday

So all the world's a
stage now. Do you
think this will be
Jake Kuhn's big chance?
Will he go on to become
a star? Laurel and
Patsy seem to think so.

"Jake's at school being Squanto, Friend of the Pilgrims," announced Patsy Kuhn when Mary Anne arrived at the Kuhns' house to baby-sit on Monday afternoon. Patsy is five.

"Mom read that to her from a book," Laurel informed me. She's six, but around Patsy she tries to act as if she is far, far older. "About Squanto."

"That's right," said Mrs. Kuhn with a smile. "Do you think you could pick him up after his rehearsal? It should be over around four-thirty."

"No problem," Mary Anne said.

But not long after Mrs. Kuhn left, Mary Anne realized that she probably wouldn't need to wait until four-thirty to go to the elementary school.

"What do you do at a reversal?" asked Patsy.

"It's not a reversal, it's a rehearsal," Laurel corrected her.

"Okay," said Patsy. She fixed her brown eyes on Mary Anne expectantly.

"You practice," Mary Anne explained. "You know, do it over and over again until you get it right."

"Like the alphabet," Patsy said, nodding.

"It's better than that," said Laurel. "Isn't it, Mary Anne?"

Mary Anne looked from one to the other. It did not take a rocket scientist to figure out the activity of choice for Patsy and Laurel that afternoon.

"Would you like to go to the school and watch your brother rehearse?"

"Yes!" both girls shrieked instantly.

"Give me five minutes and we're on our way," Mary Anne promised.

She took the five minutes to put together a mini-Kid Kit in her backpack (crayons and coloring books, a simple puzzle, a magnetic game of checkers, and a picture book featuring Big Bird). After writing Mrs. Kuhn a quick note to let her know where they were (in case Mrs. Kuhn returned early), Mary Anne took Patsy and Laurel by the hand and headed for Stoneybrook Elementary School. Both girls were tremendously excited.

"Will it be hard to find Jake?" Patsy asked. "How do you know where to go?"

"They're having the rehearsal in the auditorium," Mary Anne said. "I know where it is, because I went to school here once."

Patsy said, "I'll be in first grade next year. I'm going to be in plays and rehearse every day."

Hiding a smile at Patsy's picture of life in first grade, Mary Anne steered the girls around to the auditorium. They slipped through the rear door and settled down in seats in the back.

Mary Anne spotted me at the back of the auditorium (although I hadn't seen her yet) and pointed me out to Laurel and Patsy. At that moment, I had just spread out the big sheet of paper that was going to be the backdrop for the play. I'd drawn fir trees, and a path that disappeared into the trees. In the back corner I'd sketched one of the houses that the Pilgrims had built. On a separate sheet of posterboard, I'd drawn a picture of the *Mayflower*, on which Rebecca was working with Lindsay DeWitt.

"Claudia's in charge of the scenery," Mary Anne explained. "The kids who are helping her are called the crew. Over there in that corner, with Stacey, is the costume crew. They are working on the costumes."

"Crew," said Patsy, storing the information for future use.

Meanwhile, up on stage, Betsy's "mother" said to her, "Time to go to sleep. Tomorrow is Thanksgiving Day. Good night, Alice."

"Good night," said Betsy. She yawned and rubbed her eyes, then pretended to lie down. A moment later she sat up and frowned. "Where am I? Who are you?"

"I am Metacom," said Nicky Pike. "I am the youngest son of Massasoit, Chief of the Wampanoag. My people have come to join the Pilgrims today, for their feast of Thanksgiving."

"I am Remember Allerton," said the girl, who was really Marilyn. "I am a Pilgrim, and a Saint."

"I am Giles Hopkins," said Buddy Barrett, as the boy. "I am a Pilgrim and a Stranger." He paused and scowled. "I'd rather be a Native American."

"Whoa," said Abby. "You can't say that, Buddy. Start your speech again. And remember, Giles is a very, very important Pilgrim. A star."

Buddy looked a little happier. He delivered his speech again.

"I don't understand," said Alice. "What is a Saint? What is a Stranger?"

Remember and Giles explained to Alice that the people who had come to America on the *Mayflower* weren't all seeking religious freedom. In fact, only about a third of the voyagers were religious rebels, separatists who wanted no part of the Church of England. They called themselves Saints, after the Biblical term meaning God's chosen people. The rest of the one hundred and two people aboard the *Mayflower*, whom the Saints dubbed "Strangers," were members of the Church of England. Despite their differences, the Pilgrims, both Saints and Strangers, had decided to stick together when they had at last landed at Plymouth. They'd even drawn up an agreement called the *Mayflower* Compact. All the Saints and Strangers had voted on it and signed it — except, of course, the women and children.

"Why didn't they sign it?" asked Alice.

"Well, of course, they can't vote," said Remember, looking surprised.

"Why can't the women vote?"

"Women are the property of men," said Remember. "Women have no legal rights. They have to do what the men say. They do not vote."

"That's stupid," protested Betsy, forgetting her character.

"Betsy," said Abby warningly.

"Well, it is," said Betsy.

Suddenly Patsy shrieked, "Jake! Jake!"

Jake, who was standing near the stage, turned and waved. He trotted up the aisle. "Hi," he said to Mary Anne. "It's not time to go yet, is it? I haven't had a chance to practice my part."

"We came to watch you reverse," said Patsy.

"Rehearse," said Laurel. "Where's your costume?"

"It's not ready yet," said Jake.

Up onstage, Metacom said, "Here come my

people now. And the last of the Pautuxet people, Tisquantum, whom the Pilgrims call Squanto."

Everyone waited.

Metacom said, "*Squanto* is coming."

"Oh!" exclaimed Jake. "That's me."

He raced back up onstage to join Metacom.

"Oh, goodness," said a Pilgrim woman who had been stirring a cooking pot in the background. "There are at least ninety Wampanoag. We will have to cook much more food. Remember! Come! You must help!"

"Eighteen married women crossed the Atlantic in the *Mayflower*," said Remember to Alice. "Only six survived. There is much, much work for the women who remain!"

She hurried away.

"Let's go take our dogs and look for more crane berries," Giles said to Metacom. "That will be fun!"

The two boys hurried away. In the background, Squanto, Massasoit, Miles Standish, and the governor of the colony began to talk and gesture.

Alice suddenly exclaimed, "I know what they are talking about! The treaty they just made. We studied it in school."

Alice stopped and became Betsy. She blinked rapidly. She cleared her throat. "Treaty," she said again.

"It was a fair treaty that . . ." Abby prompted.

"It was a fair treaty that . . ." Betsy said and stopped a second time.

"Lasted more than fifty years . . ."

"Lasted more than fifty years . . ." Betsy had forgotten her lines.

"Can we paint?" asked Laurel, beginning to lose interest.

"It looks as though Claudia has plenty of help already," said Mary Anne.

"I'm a good painter," Laurel insisted, jumping to her feet as if she were about to march down the aisle and onto the stage.

Fortunately, just then Ms. Garcia looked at her watch. "Four-thirty," she announced. "Time to wrap things up. Same time, same place tomorrow."

Jake retrieved his backpack from one of the seats in the front of the auditorium, then came back to join Mary Anne and his sisters.

"You were great, Jake!" exclaimed Patsy.

"Super-duper extra-special," said Laurel. Mary Anne recognized the name of a frozen treat from a local ice-cream parlor in Laurel's description.

Jake didn't seem to mind being compared to a dish of ice cream, though. He beamed.

"I know," he said. "Squanto is the best part. His whole tribe is dead!"

"Did the Pilgrims kill them?" asked Laurel, looking worried.

"No," said Jake in the same superior, grown-up tone of voice that Laurel often used on Patsy. "They died of a sickness while Squanto was away in England, learning to speak English. The Pilgrims settled on the land where his tribe had lived. The Native Americans didn't make them move, though. They didn't believe in owning land the way the Europeans did."

Jake explained Thanksgiving all the way home, while Laurel and Patsy listened happily. (Mary Anne told me later that it was an education for her, too.) As they reached the house, Patsy announced, "I will go to first grade. And *I* will be Squanto when I grow up!"

"Me, too," said Laurel.

"Maybe you will," said Jake generously. "And if you do get the part, I'll help you rehearse."

"Thanks, Jake," said Patsy.

"Thanks," echoed Laurel.

CHAPTER 8

"Pass the pizza puh-lease," I said.

Stacey shoved the pizza across the kitchen table toward me. The Monday BSC meeting was over. On the dot of six o'clock, Kristy had herded us into the Brewer/Thomas van, and Charlie had driven us to their house, stopping to pick up a megaload of pizza on the way. Nannie, Emily Michelle, Watson, and Kristy's mom had taken their pizza into the dining room and turned the kitchen over to us. Charlie and Sam and David Michael had snagged slices and disappeared into the family room. We were crowded around the kitchen table, pigging out and talking turkey.

"Dinner for fourteen," said Kristy. "What could be easier?"

"Try adding twenty-two more people," said Stacey.

"And a few more courses," I put in.

"How many people have your parental units

had to dinner, anyway?" asked Abby, who was picking the cheese off of her pizza. "In this house?"

"Well, when Karen and Andrew are staying here, and we all eat together, there are ten of us," said Kristy. She grinned. "Not counting the ghost of Ben Brewer."

"But what about, you know, a more formal dinner?" Abby persisted.

"How formal is this Thanksgiving dinner going to be?" Mal asked, looking alarmed. "Because I don't think you can be too formal with all the kids we'll have around."

"Maybe *we* could cook Thanksgiving dinner and serve it," said Mary Anne.

"Ha." Abby snorted. "My idea of cooking is wrestling a frozen TV dinner into the microwave, not wrestling an enormous turkey into an oven. And I bet your idea of cooking, Claudia, involves unwrapping a package of something with sugar listed as the second or third ingredient."

"You mean turkey doesn't come that way?" I asked in mock surprise.

Everyone laughed.

Jessi said, "Abby's right, though. I mean, Becca and I managed to turn out a spaghetti dinner for my aunt and her un-boyfriend, back when we were trying to cook up a romance for them, but — "

72

"So we don't cook." Kristy snagged another slice of pizza.

We chewed and thought for a minute.

"Nontraditional dinner?" said Stacey.

"Explain, please," I requested.

"You know, go for something simple, like pizza. Skip the turkey and the pie and the — "

"No way!" I practically levitated. "I mean, I know that different people from different backgrounds have different foods at their Thanksgiving dinners, but I want turkey."

"Well, then, we could have someone cook it for us and just pick it up Thanksgiving morning," Stacey said.

"Sounds expensive," said Mal.

"Yup," Stacey agreed.

"Okay then, potluck," said Kristy. "That's what we'll do. It's the only logical solution. Everyone's family brings one or two dishes. And *we'll* do what we do best."

We looked at one another.

"Baby-sit," we said in unison.

Kristy nodded. "Correct. We baby-sit for all our siblings — no charge, of course — while our parents do the cooking. Plus we serve and clean up, before *and* after."

"Maid Mary Anne strikes again," muttered Mary Anne, referring to a BSC job involving a ton of housework for her.

"Yeah, but this time, we're all in it together," Kristy said.

"So now we just have to ask Watson and your mom, right?" said Jessi.

As if on cue, Kristy's mother entered the kitchen. We all became instantly (and suspiciously) silent.

"Don't let me interrupt," Mrs. Brewer said cheerfully. "I just thought I'd make some post-pizza coffee."

Immediately Kristy said, "I'll do it, Mom."

"Oh, I can do it. Thanks, though."

"No, really, Mom. Let me. I'll even bring it to you."

"Well, if you insist . . ." Mrs. Brewer gave Kristy a puzzled smile.

"Just call me Ms. Coffee," said Kristy.

The moment her mom left the kitchen, we flew into action. We didn't have to say a word to each other. Operation Serve the Coffee and Ask Kristy's Parents to Host Thanksgiving was under way.

A few minutes later, we were walking down the hall with coffee, coffee cups, sugar, a little ceramic pitcher of milk (Kristy had nuked it in the microwave, so it was hot), and real napkins.

"Goodness," said Kristy's mom as we walked into the dining room.

Watson dabbed his mouth with his napkin.

I *think* he was hiding a smile. Nannie raised her eyebrows. Emily kept mashing a mushroom with her spoon.

We served them coffee with a flourish.

"Anything else?" asked Kristy when we were through.

Her grandmother looked up with a twinkle in her eye. "I have a feeling there might be."

The three adults exchanged glances. Then they looked back at Kristy.

"Okay, okay, this is the deal," said Kristy. "We think Thanksgiving should be a really big celebration this year. You know, friends as well as family. Everybody all together."

"Everybody who?" said Watson, stirring his coffee.

"Well, you know, the Stevensons' plans to go to Long Island fell through," said Kristy.

"We're not going to New York, either," said Mal.

"My mom and dad mixed up their schedules," put in Stacey, "so she and I are going to be alone in Stoneybrook."

Watson raised his hand. "Hold it — let me guess. *Everybody's* Thanksgiving plans fell through."

"Yes. So we thought maybe we could have Thanksgiving together, all of us and all our families. Here," Kristy finished up.

Watson and Mrs. Brewer looked around the

dining room in a dazed sort of way.

"It's only thirty-six people," said Kristy.

Nannie snorted and quickly raised her coffee cup to her lips to stifle her laughter.

We waited for the adults to freak out.

But Watson just said slowly, "Could we even seat thirty-six people in this dining room? I think this table only expands to seat twelve."

"Not all in the dining room," Kristy said. "We thought we could set up other tables, too. In the living room, and maybe in the library. The little kids could eat at the kitchen table. We'd just be sort of spread out."

Watson began to smile. "It'll be a madhouse."

"A total madhouse," agreed Kristy's mom.

"It will be a *very* organized madhouse," Kristy said. She explained the potluck cooking with free baby-sitting plan, emphasizing the before-and-after cleanup services.

"Well, you can pull it off if anybody can," said Nannie.

"I say we go for it," said Watson. He and Kristy's mom exchanged a big smile.

"Provided everyone's parents agree," added Kristy's mom.

Kristy pumped her fist in the air. "All *right!*"

We made a mad dash for the Brewer/ Thomas phone, Watson's business phone, and his fax phone (Abby's mother was still at work in New York, so Watson said we could fax her), and had our invitations out in no time. Our guest list looked like this:

Me, Janine, my mom and dad;

Kristy, her mom, her stepfather, Nannie, Charlie, Sam, David Michael, and Emily Michelle;

Abby, Anna, and their mom;

Jessi, Becca, Squirt, Mr. Ramsey, Mrs. Ramsey, and Aunt Cecelia;

Stacey and her mom;

Mary Anne, her dad, and her stepmom;

Mallory, her mom and dad, Byron, Adam, Jordan, Vanessa, Nicky, Margo, and Claire.

We had invited thirty-six people to Thanksgiving dinner at Kristy's house and thirty-six people accepted — including ourselves, of course.

Not including the ghost of Ben Brewer!

CHAPTER 9

By Tuesday afternoon, *Alice and the Pilgrims* was taking shape. The scenery and costumes were looking good, and the kids had studied their lines the night before. Clearly, they were very excited about the play.

It was also clear that their parents were involved. Not only were they helping their budding stage stars learn lines, but some of them had even showed up for rehearsal. A couple of teachers stayed late to watch, too. The enthusiasm was nice.

At least, that's what I thought at first.

The crew had finished the drawing of the *Mayflower*. To make "water" for it, we spread half-folded and crumpled old navy blue sheets with some artistically arranged white and lighter blue streamers across the front of the stage. We still hadn't achieved the exact effect we wanted, but we were working on it.

Just then, a boy named Tyson, who was the

narrator, came onstage and stood in front of the curtain. He pushed his glasses up and peered out at the audience, then peered down at the piece of paper in his hand.

"The Pilgrims were English men and women," he announced. He stopped. He cleared his throat. "The Pilgrims were English men and women. They boarded a ship called the *Mayflower* and sailed across the ocean for over sixty days, until they reached this country. They landed on Plymouth Rock. They built their houses on land that belonged to the Native Americans. They were very strict and very religious. Our play is called *Alice and the Pilgrims*. It is the story of the first Thanksgiving."

Behind Tyson, two third-graders (who would be dressed in Pilgrim costumes on the evening of the play) came out holding the *Mayflower* poster. They rocked it up and down above the blue sheets and streamers as they "sailed" it back and forth across the stage.

Then I heard Rick hiss, "Curtain! Help me raise the curtain."

Slowly the curtain came up as the *Mayflower* "sailed" offstage.

Alice went to sleep, and woke up in Plymouth to meet Giles, Metacom, and Remember.

Squanto and Miles Standish had a fight.

Needless to say, that wasn't in the script.

It started when Miles stepped on Squanto's foot.

"Oww!" howled Jake.

"What happened?" Abby said.

"She stomped my toes."

"Why aren't you wearing shoes?" Abby asked.

"Because I'm Squanto," Jake said. "It's part of my costume."

"This isn't a dress rehearsal," said Abby. "Put your shoes on. And," she added, before Jake could argue, "even if it was a dress rehearsal, and you were in costume, your costume would include moccasins, because that's what the Native Americans wore during cold weather."

"Ha!" said Carolyn.

"Double ha," said Jake. "Get off my land, you, you, ugly Pilgrim."

"It isn't your land," said Carolyn, stomping her foot.

"Is too."

"Is not!"

"S'too."

"S'not."

"Snot."

"Stew!" shrieked Carolyn, going off into gales of laughter.

"Snot stew snot stew," chanted Jake.

That stopped the play. It took a few minutes to restore order.

Meanwhile, my crew and I finished painting the trees on the backdrop.

"We should sign it," said Charlotte.

A little girl named Susie Albion said, "We can't. It would look silly. Wouldn't it, Claudia?"

I held my paintbrush in the air thoughtfully. I was remembering a cement sidewalk, long ago. It was fresh, new cement. I saw Kristy and Mary Anne and me, age five, bending over to plant our hands in that wet cement while my grandmother Mimi watched and nodded.

We'd signed the sidewalk with our handprints back then. Why couldn't we sign the backdrop with our handprints now?

"Wait a minute," I said, "I have an idea."

Suddenly Susie said, "Oh, look. There's Mommy! May I go say hello, Claudia?"

"Sure," I said. I glanced over my shoulder and saw that a couple more adults had arrived. A man with a ruddy face was talking to a woman with a pinched mouth who was nodding like a puppet at every word he said.

They both looked toward the stage.

I smiled at them.

They frowned ferociously.

It made me feel weird. Then I saw Susie talking to the woman with the pinched mouth. The woman scowled and pointed at *me*.

How rude!

I turned my back on them and bent over one end of a long sheet of paper. I began to draw.

"There!" I said at last, stepping back so the crew could see what I'd done.

"It's just a plain old brown tree," said Becca.

"It's more than that," I told her and the other kids standing there. "It's a secret signature tree."

Just then, Susie ran back to me.

"Is everything okay?" I couldn't help asking.

Susie nodded. "Mommy just wanted to know what we were painting. I told her, trees. She asked me if I was sure that was *all* we were painting."

I wondered what Susie's mom had thought we were painting. Naked Pilgrims?

"How is it a secret tree?" asked Charlotte.

"Watch," I said. I laid down a spare piece of posterboard. Carefully, I poured little puddles of orange, yellow, brown, and red paint on it. I bent over and pressed my hand into a puddle of red paint, then turned and pressed it against our backdrop. It looked as if my red handprint was attached to one of the smaller branches of the tree.

"See? We'll make leaves out of our handprints, with all the autumn colors. Those will be our secret signatures."

"Cool," said Susie. She bent over and went to work.

In no time at all we had a very leafy "signed" tree in one corner of our backdrop.

As we finished, I realized that the rehearsal was coming to an end. The kids washed their hands, then helped me put the paint away and wash the brushes. I sat down at the edge of the stage, feeling tired, but satisfied with the afternoon's work.

"Cool," a voice echoed Susie's word. It was Stacey.

"We like it," I said. "Whew. My back hurts from bending over this art stuff."

"Why don't you just kneel or something?" asked Stacey.

"I did." I pointed to smudges of paint on the knees of my jeans. Fortunately, they were old jeans that I had brought to school and changed into just for painting the backdrop.

"How're the costumes coming?" I asked.

"Well, Erica and I have managed to convince the kids that the Pilgrims didn't all wear somber black clothing. But they're just not buying the idea that the Native Americans didn't wear huge war bonnets all the time."

I giggled. Our research had turned up some good drawings of what the Pilgrims and Native Americans had worn — along with the news that none of the tribes east of the Mississippi wore feathered headdresses. At the most, the men would wear single feathers in their hair.

"Wait till we start painting the feast," I said. "And I tell them no pumpkin pie, or half the other stuff that most of them think of as Thanksgiving food."

"And don't forget the raw oysters," added Stacey.

"Ewww, don't remind me," I said. But it was true. We'd discovered that oysters were probably part of that first Thanksgiving feast. Not oyster dressing, just oysters.

"Let's go," said Stacey.

Most of the other kids were on their way out, with their parents or with baby-sitters. I couldn't help noticing that Mrs. Albion wasn't the only unhappy-looking parent. It didn't make me feel good.

Ms. Garcia was standing by the back door of the auditorium as Stacey and I walked out. She was talking with an intense-looking man I recognized as one of the third-grade teachers.

"Of course that's not what we're trying to

do. My Short Takes students have done their research and it is one hundred percent accurate," I heard her say.

" 'Bye, Ms. Garcia," I said as we walked by her.

" 'Bye," echoed Stacey.

Ms. Garcia broke off what she was saying and gave us a distracted smile. " 'Night," she said. "See you tomorrow."

The other teacher didn't say anything.

But I sure didn't like the way he glanced at us as we left. Thank goodness I wasn't in third grade anymore! He looked like a real crank.

CHAPTER 10

Wednesday

Becca's been totally into the scenery for the third grade play, and so has Charlotte. So I was glad that my baby-sitting job for Charlotte started with picking her up after rehearsal. I wanted to see how the play was going. And did I ever!!!!

Jessi arrived at the SES auditorium half an hour early to see our next rehearsal. She had planned on slipping in quietly, so as not to distract the kids, and sitting in the back of the auditorium.

But when she pushed open the rear door of the auditorium, she found the auditorium anything but quiet.

It was at least half filled with parents and teachers. Some of them were sitting in the chairs. Some of them were standing in clumps up and down the aisles. Some were talking. Others were listening, leaning forward to peer at the third-graders onstage as they said their lines.

At first Jessi thought she'd encountered a severe and massive attack of Stage Parent-itis: parents who are convinced and determined that their kids are going to be Stars.

She wondered if some of the parents were going to complain that their kids hadn't gotten roles, or maybe that their parts weren't big enough. Smiling to herself, Jessi found a seat.

She spotted her sister busily painting on a long sheet of paper. From the colors being splashed around, she deduced that they were probably working on the sky. She and Charlotte were kneeling next to each other, concentrating hard and working furiously.

"What do you mean, women get to vote?" the Pilgrim girl named Remember said to Betsy. "Women aren't allowed to vote!"

"Women finally won the right to vote in nineteen twenty-one," said Betsy. "But they still don't have equal rights. That's a law that hasn't been passed yet."

"This is outrageous," a red-haired woman sitting in front of Jessi said to the tall woman in the seat next to her.

Jessi frowned and leaned forward slightly to listen.

"It certainly is," said the tall one.

The play continued. And with each point Betsy or one of the other characters made about the differences between things then and now, more angry murmurs seemed to fill the air. Jessi began to realize that people were objecting to the play's points about women, sex roles, and the role of the European settlers.

Jessi was alarmed at how angry and hateful they sounded. And she was truly amazed at how ignorant and narrow-minded people's comments were.

Up onstage, Betsy, in the role of Alice, turned to face the audience. "Not everyone celebrates Thanksgiving in this country," she said. "Some Wampanoags and other Native Americans come to Plymouth Rock on Thanksgiving Day now to hold a National Day of Mourning. For them, the first Thanksgiving marked the beginning of the end of their way of life, even though their ancestors didn't know that when they welcomed the religious refugees from Europe."

"Stop!" a voice suddenly called from one side of the auditorium. "Stop this instant. This is un-American!"

The auditorium seemed to freeze. Onstage, Betsy stood with her mouth open. Some of the other actors drew closer together, as if they were afraid.

Bright red flooded Ms. Garcia's cheeks. And Abby's, too. (She had been prompting Betsy.)

"Un-American!" the voice repeated, and a third grade teacher marched forward and up onto the stage.

The spell was broken. Enthusiastic shouts and applause came from the adults in the auditorium.

By now, the children looked scared and confused.

The auditorium seemed to burst with activity and noise. Parents joined the teacher on the stage. The voices rose louder and louder.

Jessi jumped to her feet, not sure what to do. Then she began to push forward, hoping to rescue Becca and Charlotte from the melee.

"Well, I think it's disrespectful of *you* to interrupt like that," she heard Abby retort.

"Let's calm down," Ms. Garcia said. "If we discuss this calmly — "

The third-grade teacher, who was standing in the middle of the stage waving his arms, turned to Ms. Garcia. "The time for discussion has passed," he snapped.

"What kind of nonsense is this?" said someone else. "The Pilgrims were heroes. They came to a savage, uncivilized country and made something of it."

"Oh, yeah?" Abby shouted. "Tell that to the Native Americans! And then ask the Pilgrims what they believed about Jews. Europe wasn't civilized, it was bigoted and prejudiced. Just because you believe a bunch of lies and propaganda doesn't mean we have to!"

Jessi was stunned. The anger in the room seemed to explode. She half expected Abby to get arrested or something, right then and there.

She forced her way through the screaming, gesturing crowd of parents, and found a group of kids huddled in one corner of the stage with Stacey.

"Stacey!" she gasped. "Can't anybody do anything?"

"Lay low," said Stacey. "That's my advice."

Looking around, Jessi realized that not all the parents of all the third-graders were there. Her own parents certainly weren't. Neither were Charlotte's. Nor were kids from the Pike, Dewitt, Kuhn, Arnold, and Hobart families being held by the arm while their mothers or fathers raged about the un-American play.

Jessi was relieved. For a moment, she felt a little better.

"Hi," she said to the kids.

"Hi," said Carolyn. She scowled. "Does this mean I can't be Miles Standish?"

"Of course not," said Stacey quickly. But as Jessi told me later, Stacey didn't sound all that confident.

Becca and Charlotte ran to Jessi then. "Jessi, why is everybody so mad?" asked Becca.

"They're scared," said Jessi. "It's easier for them to believe fiction than fact."

"What?" asked Charlotte.

"Never mind," said Jessi. "Where's Claudia, Stace?"

"I don't know. She was here a minute ago."

"She went to put away the art supplies," said Jake. "She said it didn't look as if we were going to need them anymore today."

Jessi said to Stacey, "Well, I think we better head out of here. See you later."

"Okay," said Stacey.

Taking her younger sister and Charlotte by the hand, Jessi began to lead them off the stage and out of the auditorium. Everywhere she looked, angry faces turned toward her. Angry voices flew over her head.

"Just ignore them," she said in a low voice to Becca and Charlotte.

They stepped out of the auditorium and found me, staring up at the sky. Why was I staring at it? I don't know. Maybe I thought some kind of answer would drop out of the clouds.

I should have known it wouldn't. I've tried the same thing during tests a hundred times and never once has the answer come to me that way.

"Wow," said Jessi.

"Yeah," I said.

"What's going to happen?" Jessi asked me.

"Will we still have a play?" asked Becca.

I looked down at Becca and Charlotte. They'd worked so hard. But if I said yes and then the play didn't go on, that would make me a liar — and make them twice as disappointed.

"I don't know," I said gently. "Maybe. Maybe not."

"But we haven't finished painting the sky,"

Charlotte protested. "We're going to do that tomorrow, aren't we?"

I sighed. I looked up at the clouds again. Still no answer.

"I don't know," I told them. "We'll just have to wait and see."

CHAPTER 11

Did I worry all that night? I did.

Was I completely tied up in knots by the time I reached my Short Takes class the next day?

I was.

It didn't help that the whole school seemed to have heard about the Big Thanksgiving Fight. I tried to follow Stacey's advice, to lay low and give vague answers to anyone who asked.

Ms. Garcia was standing by her desk as we entered the room. Needless to say, none of us was late. We sat down without saying a word and faced Ms. Garcia. She looked gravely back at us.

When the bell rang, signaling the beginning of class, she said, "I'm afraid I have some bad news."

No one groaned or gasped. Somehow, no one was surprised.

"They killed our play, didn't they?" asked Rick.

"Not exactly," said Ms. Garcia. "But we have been given an ultimatum by the principal of Stoneybrook Elementary School, at the behest of the majority of her third-grade teachers, and quite a few of her third-graders' parents. Either put on a play that shows the traditional first Thanksgiving story, or the principal will, er, kill the play."

Abby exclaimed, "That's censorship!"

Erica asked, "Can they do that?"

"I believe it is censorship, too, Abby. And yes, Erica, they can do that," Ms. Garcia answered.

"What about our freedom of speech?" someone else said. "Or is that some made-up part of our history, too, just like Thanksgiving?"

"Wait a minute," I objected. "Thanksgiving is not made up. It's just been polished, and the parts that people don't want to know about have been left out most of the time."

Fourteen pairs of eyes looked questioningly at me — including Stacey's.

"It's true," I said.

"It is true," agreed Ms. Garcia. "We have been told the truth about Thanksgiving. Just not the whole truth."

"It's all in who tells the story," said Rick.

"That's one way of looking at it," agreed Ms. Garcia.

"It's still censorship, to say we have to tell the story their way," said Abby.

Ms. Garcia said, "Someone, I don't remember who right now, once said, 'I don't agree with what you say, but I'll defend to the death your right to say it.' That's at the core of one of our constitutional rights, the right to freedom of speech. And do remember," she went on, "that the people who *object* to our play have a right to freedom of speech, too. Freedom of speech applies to everyone, and to all views."

"The price of freedom is eternal vigilance," said Abby suddenly. "That's a quote from Thomas Jefferson, I think. But even if it's not, it's still true. If we give in, we're not being vigilant. And we lose freedom."

Ms. Garcia folded her arms and leaned back. "It's up to you. You can cancel the play. Or the show can go on — rewritten."

"Kill it," said Abby instantly. "Don't give in! Then maybe when the narrow-minded parents and teachers see how disappointed the third-graders are, they'll be the ones who give in."

"I don't think that's going to happen," said Ms. Garcia.

Rick said, "Then we just don't do it and that's that."

We sat with the idea a moment. Finally I said, "If we do that — if we kill the play in protest — it really is going to disappoint a lot of little kids. And they've worked very hard on the scenery and the costumes already."

"They *are* awfully excited," someone else agreed.

Rick said slowly, "I can see the parents' point of view, in a way. I mean, I bet at least some of them think that by censoring our play, they're protecting their kids."

"Also, they might never have heard some of the things we were saying in our play," said Erica. "When they were growing up, people probably didn't even know what rights for women and minorities were. This probably scares them. Hey, *we* didn't know a lot of this stuff before we started our research."

"True," said Abby reluctantly. "And if they'd asked us to change some things about the play, or even tried to talk to us about it, we might have compromised. But I think what they're doing now is wrong."

"So what do we do? Put on the play *their* way?" said Stacey, frowning.

"But that's giving in to them," I said. "We can't just give up."

Ms. Garcia looked at the clock. "The bell is going to ring in ten minutes. I'll need a decision by the end of class."

"I guess we have to take a vote," said Abby. "All in favor . . . wait a minute! I have an idea. What if we put the play on under protest?"

"What do you mean?" I asked.

"We agree to the traditional version, but we make it clear that we've been forced to give in, that we've been censored."

"Deprived of our freedom of speech!" cried Erica.

"We can stamp 'Censored' in big red letters across all the posters and playbills," I said.

"And wear buttons," said Stacey. "Buttons that say things like, 'The censors made me do it' and 'Ask me what happened at the first Thanksgiving.' "

"And we could also put the original play on ourselves at SMS," I said, warming to the idea. *The* True *Story of Alice and the Pilgrims.*"

The bell rang. It was the end of class.

"Everybody in favor of two plays raise your hand," said Ms. Garcia quickly. It was unanimous.

We had only just begun to fight!

CHAPTER 12

The Monday evening before Thanksgiving arrived. Opening night — and closing night — for our censored play. Despite the fact that parents had been at every rehearsal watching us like hawks, especially Mrs. Albion, who was convinced that there was some kind of sinister meaning behind our tree of hands — we'd managed to preserve some of the interesting things, such as the food being different at the first Thanksgiving. And we managed to keep the costumes accurate.

Since Betsy couldn't be Alice anymore, we'd given her the role of Governor William Bradford, who hadn't had a speaking part in the original play. I think the father of one of the boys who didn't have a speaking part protested to Ms. Garcia about that. At least, I saw him frowning and gesturing toward the stage when Betsy first began to rehearse her new part. I don't know what Ms. Garcia said to him, but she definitely didn't give in.

We'd made posters and given them to the third-graders to put up at SES. I'd kept the design of the posters simple — just a black and white silhouette of the *Mayflower*, with block style printing about the play. The word "Censored," in big, red letters, would show up very well against it.

During one BSC meeting, we had made buttons while we answered the phone. We came up with some pretty good slogans: "The price of freedom of speech is eternal vigilance" was one. "Native Americans for the Real Thanksgiving" was another. "Thanksgiving then, Thanksgiving now — where are the women?" (That was Abby's.) Also: "Were the Pilgrims against freedom of speech?"; "Narrow-minded, racist, sexist, CENSORED"; "Whose play is this anyway?"; "The truth about Thanksgiving has been canceled by the parents and teachers of SES"; "*Alice and the Pilgrims* — CENSORED." We also made lots of buttons that just said, "Censored."

We wrote "Censored" in red marker on the front of every single one of the playbills. Rick had designed the playbills on his computer. He had printed the title of our play, *Alice and the Pilgrims*, at the top. "Censored" went across that. Below it, in block letters, were the words, "A Thanksgiving Play." We also made up fliers announcing the performance of the original play on Tuesday night at SMS.

Mal had told her family about the controversy, and her family was planning to turn out with buttons on. So was Jessi's. Kristy and Charlie and Sam were going, bringing David Michael and Emily Michelle. Abby's sister Anna was coming, along with some of her friends from the orchestra. So no matter what happened, at least some people would be on our side.

Everyone in my Short Takes class arrived at the auditorium extra early. We raced around writing "Censored" across all the posters. I felt as if I were writing graffiti. I want to point out, though, that I was a very well-dressed graffiti artist/protestor. Just for the occasion, I was wearing my rainbow-colored crinkle gauze skirt, my crocheted vest with the matching hat, and my silver earrings (designed by me, of course). I felt that I looked artistic, yet responsible. And of course my button, with the bright red writing on it, added the finishing touch.

We'd asked the kids to "sign in" backstage, so most of them arrived by the backstage door. We'd arranged it that way because it was easier — and because it meant that the parents who arrived with the kids wouldn't see the posters right away, and wouldn't have time (we hoped) to do anything awful.

The third-graders were tremendously excited. Most of them had put on their costumes at home and there were a few surprises. Carolyn Arnold had found out that one of Miles Standish's contemporaries had described him as having red hair. Somewhere she'd come up with a red wig, which she was wearing beneath her black hat. My lips twitched when I saw her, because the wig was a curly one. But I didn't say anything.

Betsy was wearing a big black mustache. (I couldn't help thinking of the Pike kids, all dressed like Groucho Marx on Halloween.) But since we didn't know exactly what any of the Pilgrims had looked like (there were no photographs, and only one contemporary portrait), what difference did it make?

"Nice mustache," I told Betsy. She beamed. She had been a little upset about losing the role of Alice, but being the governor and wearing a mustache seemed to have made up for it.

Just then I heard someone screech, "You're killing the turkey!"

I left Betsy and hurried off to separate two Pilgrims who were engaged in a sword fight, using two cardboard turkey drumsticks. Carefully I reattached the drumsticks to the papier-mâché turkey that was sitting on the picnic table we were using for the Pilgrims' feast table.

After that, I hurried around, giving the scenery last-minute adjustments, and making sure the bowl of real cranberries we'd put on the table didn't become part of a real food fight.

I didn't have time to think about the potentially unfriendly audience that was gathering outside. Briefly, I realized that I was glad we had decided to go on with the censored play. The kids were having so much fun that the play's content almost didn't seem to matter.

Then Abby said, "Places everyone! Five minutes to curtain."

A shrill babble of third-grade voices rose. "Shhh!" we said, but in vain. It was all we could do to hustle everyone to their spots and keep them standing still until, at last, the curtain began to rise.

I pushed a plate of oyster shells, arranged to look like real oysters on the half shell (yuk), away from the edge of the table and darted offstage.

"A Thanksgiving Play" had begun.

Walking to center stage front, Tyson made a speech introducing the play. Behind him, another third-grader walked across the stage, holding the *Mayflower* poster to show the ship sailing across the "sea" of blue sheets and blue and white streamers.

"How'd it go out front?" I asked Rick. He'd been helping the third-grade ushers, who were handing out programs and escorting people to their seats.

"Do the words 'outrage' and 'disgrace' mean anything to you?" asked Rick wryly.

"They weren't happy about the 'Censored' treatment, I guess."

"Nope. But it was too late for them to do anything more than complain. At least half a dozen of them asked who was responsible for this. I told them that they could find our names on the backs of their programs."

I gave a smothered snort of laughter. But I was secretly glad that I hadn't been there to hear it.

So the play went on. The kids enjoyed it tremendously. Jake waved at his parents from the stage.

Betsy twirled her mustache, and welcomed Massasoit and his people to the Thanksgiving feast. Jake, as Squanto, overacted all over the place, turning and grinning and waving at the audience, and bowing whenever he finished "translating" the low, indistinguishable words that the chief whispered into his ear.

It was a nice, traditional version of the first

Thanksgiving. By the time the play was over, and it was clear that we'd given the audience what they'd wanted and not the whole truth, the grumbling had subsided. The kids took their bows to steady applause. Cameras flashed, and faces beamed.

The applause slackened as Ms. Garcia announced our names, but since we came out with the groups of third-graders we'd worked with, and took bows with them, the parents couldn't not applaud.

But they couldn't miss the buttons we were wearing, either.

Even though the applause for us was dutiful at best, I didn't mind. As we were cleaning up after the play, and discussing the production of our own version the following night at SMS, I was still glad we'd decided to go through with it. We'd managed to keep the parents at bay and the third-graders happy. And we'd managed to stand up for our beliefs.

It had been a good evening's work.

CHAPTER 13

When the parents and teachers of SES had censored our play and we'd decided to do our own version of the Thanksgiving story, *Alice and the Pilgrims*, we'd recruited the Short Takes class that was concentrating on performance to put on the uncensored "Alice" play. Needless to say, they'd welcomed the idea, and before we knew it, they were immersed in it. The only work we had to do was to preview the dress rehearsal and show up for the performance on Tuesday night.

There's usually a decent turnout for school plays at SMS, but they're not the most wildly popular activity around. I'd expected friends and loyal supporters, the kids in our classes, and maybe a few of the curious who'd heard about the censorship rumble.

Wrong.

A seething mass of parents and even some

SES teachers showed up. They weren't wearing buttons, but obviously our buttons and "Censored" signs the previous evening had made a big impression.

They were, to put it mildly, angry that we'd stood up to them.

The play was scheduled to start at eight o'clock. We planned to arrive at seven-thirty to make sure we'd find good seats.

I guess you could say that the picket line was the first thing that alerted us to the fact that finding good seats might not be our biggest worry.

The BSC had turned out in force, including Shannon and Logan. We were in the Brewer/Thomas van, which Charlie was driving. Behind us, Watson was driving Nannie, Kristy's mom, and Sam, David Michael, and Emily Michelle in his car.

Charlie pulled the van up to the front entrance of SMS and slowed to a stop, whistling. "Would you look at that?" he said.

There was a picket line in front of the school. Dozens of parents with set, angry faces were marching up and down, holding signs that said things such as, "Un-American," and "We're for Family Values — and the American Thanksgiving."

"Ick," said Mary Anne.

"Ick?" teased Logan. *"Ick?"*

"Ick, sick," said Kristy emphatically. Then she pointed. "Look!"

Another group of protestors, who looked equally grim, marched back and forth, never looking at the first group of protestors. This bunch held signs that said, "Hatred of the truth is not a family value," and "Freedom of speech is a constitutional right."

Of course, *we* were wearing our "Censored" buttons. Easy to tell which side we were on.

I swallowed. "Think that first group will hit us in the head with their signs?"

I was only half kidding.

"Come on," said Kristy. "Thanks for the ride, Charlie. See you inside."

She leaped from the van. Abby was right behind her. Then we just stood there.

"Smile, and don't look so worried," Kristy ordered.

So we smiled. And ran the gauntlet of people saying to us, "You ought to be ashamed of yourselves," and, "Disgraceful."

Abby turned. We could tell she was about to say something really outrageous back to them. Kristy grabbed her and we hustled her forward.

Then I heard another voice say, "Good work! We're proud of you."

And then we were through the front doors.

But it wasn't over yet. Inside, people on both sides of the issue were handing out literature about education and censorship and even something called a "Secret Agenda to Corrupt Young Minds."

I wanted to take one of those, to see if I'd been corrupted, but Kristy kept us moving. Before we knew it, we were sitting in the middle of a row near the front of the auditorium.

"I'm not sure I want to sit with my back to so many people who don't like me," I said.

Stacey snickered.

As it turned out, we were joined soon after by Kristy's family. Then the Pikes arrived in force. Soon we were surrounded by supporters.

I couldn't believe our little play had become such a big civil rights issue.

At 8:07, Mr. Taylor, the SMS principal, strode onstage and announced our play. As the curtains rose, many people applauded. And many people booed.

That was just the beginning. Whenever the eighth-grader playing Alice began to speak, people began to clap. And boo. It grew so loud that often she was drowned out.

Finally she put her hands on her hips and just stood there, staring at the audience.

Things quieted down for a moment. Then people began to murmur and whisper, and you could tell it was going to start all over again.

But Mr. Taylor acted quickly. He strode out onto the stage to stand beside the actress. He looked angry.

"That's enough!" he said in the same tone of voice that he uses with rowdy students.

Many of the parents must have recognized that tone from their own childhoods. Silence fell.

"If you cannot behave while these students perform, you will be asked to leave the auditorium. You are more than welcome to exercise your right to freedom of speech, and to protest as you see fit — outside this auditorium. But coming inside means that you will abide by the rules of common courtesy. Now be quiet!"

He strode off stage. I wanted to applaud, but I was afraid to make a sound!

After that, the play went smoothly, although from time to time you could hear angry murmurs in the darkness around us.

Once things had quieted down and I could pay attention to the play, I began to notice something. Without the third-graders looking cute and charming, and obviously getting a big kick out of being in costume and up on a stage, the play didn't seem as good. As it went on, I was forced to admit that, well, it simply

110

wasn't a very good play. What did I expect? It had been written quickly, and for a third-grade level. If this had been a Broadway production, I thought wryly, we might not have been censored, but the critics probably would have given us such bad reviews that we would have closed on opening night!

When the play was over, my friends and I jumped to our feet and began to applaud and cheer as loudly as we could. Ms. Garcia came onstage and called our Short Takes class up to join the performers.

The applause sounded thunderous from there. But as loud as it was, it didn't drown out the chorus of boos from the opposition.

With the sound rolling over us, Erica and I ducked offstage. We returned with a huge bouquet of red roses, which we gave to Ms. Garcia.

More applause.

More boos.

Then Ms. Garcia did an amazing thing. She turned and walked toward our class, and handed each of us a rose from her bouquet.

We took a final bow.

But we didn't stay to chat. We ducked out the side door of the stage to avoid the pickets and the arguing that began to fill the air the moment the curtain fell.

That night, before I went to bed, I decided

to dry the rose. I laid the playbill out on the desk, along with some of the notes I'd taken about Thanksgiving. A collage was taking shape in my mind.

I didn't go to sleep right away. My thoughts drifted back to my "Learning to Read" Short Takes class. I wondered how much of history had been censored, how many other things that the people in charge didn't like had been edited out of the history books.

History was like that, I realized. There was nothing simple about it. In the end, it was a complicated mix of truth and fiction. A matter of interpretation. You couldn't believe everything you read — or were told.

It made the whole world seem a lot more complicated.

I wondered, just before I fell into a deep sleep, whether the people who'd censored our play and tried to prevent us from exercising our freedom of speech, realized that the only reason they could protest at all was because of the same right to freedom of speech they'd tried to deny us.

It made the world seem a lot more complicated.

CHAPTER 14

Wenesday

Atenshun, all Baby-siters Club clints!
We do parteis. Big parties. Big, big
parteis. Like thankgiving for 36 peple...

Wednesday was what you might call School Lite. Everyone was looking forward to the holidays. Many of the teachers let their classes have free periods or hold small Thanksgiving celebrations. They didn't even give out homework assignments.

In Short Takes, we spent the entire class debating what had happened, how much freedom of speech the Bill of Rights guaranteed, and what it all meant. And we congratulated ourselves a lot, too.

School let out at noon. Whatever the controversies surrounding Thanksgiving, it is an excellent holiday in terms of length!

But I didn't plan to lounge around in my room eating Twinkies and talking on the phone to Stacey. Instead I dashed home (just like the other members of the BSC), pitched my books, and headed for Mal's.

At one o'clock, baby-sitters and their brothers and sisters began arriving. Mal's was the designated baby-sitting drop-off point for everyone, while our parents, plus Nannie and Jessi's aunt Cecelia, cooked up a storm over at Kristy's house.

We had chosen the Pikes' because it's pretty kid-proof already, and because Mr. and Mrs. Pike had suggested it.

What did we do with all those kids? What

good baby-sitters do, of course. We kept them busy and happy. We had a lot of help, too, from some honorary baby-sitters: Charlie, Sam, Janine, and Anna had volunteered to help out.

"Who wants to make Thanksgiving cookies?" asked Abby. She opened a paper bag and spilled out about a dozen cookie cutters.

"Wowwwww," breathed Margo Pike. "Look, Claire," she said to her little sister. "There's a Pilgrim's hat."

"And a turkey," said Claire. "No, two turkeys. A big one and a little one."

"And a pumpkin," said Nicky.

"That one is supposed to be a Pilgrim woman," said Anna. "And that one is a Pilgrim man. You have to decorate them, though, to see what they really look like."

"Where did you get all these?" asked Jessi.

"They were our father's. He liked to make cookies," Anna said. "He used to make us Thanksgiving cookies. We'd — "

"So who's going to help us?" Abby suddenly interrupted. I wondered if talking about her father bothered her, or if she was just being typically Abby.

"I want to make cookies," said David Michael.

"Me, too," said Vanessa.

"Cookie," said Emily Michelle.

"That's too bad," said Mary Anne. "I guess I'm going to have to make Thanksgiving decorations for Kristy's house all by myself. I don't know how I'm ever going to use up all those different colored pieces of paper and all that glitter and — "

"I want to make decorations," said David Michael.

"You," said Mal, fixing her triplet brothers with a steely glare, "have to clean your room before you do anything."

A wail of protest went up from Byron, Adam, and Jordan. That's when Charlie and Sam stepped in and organized a turkey hunt. Sam folded up a dollar bill into an origami turkey (which caused Kristy to look at him in surprise — clearly her older brother had talents of which she hadn't been aware). Then he and Charlie hid the turkey. The only clue Sam offered them was, "You'll have to clean your room to find it."

In no time at all we could hear thumps and bumps from their room. Meanwhile, Charlie and Sam returned, and Charlie started making cranberry sauce.

"Where'd you hide it?" I asked.

Sam began to snicker. "Someplace it'll take them forever to find." He walked across the kitchen and into the pantry. Emerging a moment later he said, "I taped it to the handle of the broom in the pantry!"

Claire insisted on giving all her cookies cranberry eyes. They were sort of strange-looking.

"Did you know that the Native Americans used to call cranberries 'ibimi,' which meant bitter berry?" I asked, imagining the sour taste of the cranberry eyes with the different flavors of the cookies. It didn't slow Claire down one bit. In fact, she tasted a cranberry and said, "It's not so bitter."

Vanessa switched from cookies to place mats. Soon she and Sam were making up poems to go on the place mats. Jessi put Squirt and Emily Michelle down for a nap. A moment later, the triplets dashed into the kitchen. "Our room is clean," announced Byron in an aggrieved voice. "And we still haven't found the turkey."

"Is your room really clean?" asked Mal. "Did you make up your beds and dust off the shelves and sweep the floors?"

The triplets disappeared again.

"You gave it away, Mal," said Jessi.

"Yup. But they'll make their beds and dust before they think about the broom."

Over by the stove, Charlie snickered.

"Listen," commanded Vanessa. She held up a place mat with a turkey drawing. "I am not last, I am not least, I am the turkey of the feast."

My sister burst out laughing. "That sounds like one of your puns, Claudia."

I looked at her in surprise. Then I grinned.

"What are you laughing at?" Vanessa asked in surprise.

"Over to you, Janine," I said.

The triplets thundered back into the room. For a moment, as they all tried to wedge themselves in the door at once, I thought the door frame was going to come out. Then Adam popped free and shot across the kitchen and into the pantry.

"I won! I won!" he cried, emerging with the broom held aloft.

"Do we still have to sweep our room?" asked Byron, looking disgruntled.

"What do you think?" asked Mal.

"Can we play a game afterward?"

"Sure," said Mal.

The door frame shuddered under the impact once more and then they were gone.

We played pin-the-tail-on-the-turkey when they came back. (I had drawn a big picture of a turkey, and we made tails out of construction paper.) Fortunately, one wall of the Pikes' family room is completely covered in cork, so it didn't matter where the thumbtacks went in the wall.

Abby and Anna had just taken the cookies out of the oven when a loud wail announced that Squirt was awake.

"I'll get him," I volunteered, heading for the bedroom where he'd been sleeping. I picked up Squirt, who was rubbing his eyes, and checked on Emily. She was still asleep, but then she'd had practice sleeping while a large family was in high gear around her.

"Can he have some juice now?" I asked Jessi, returning to the kitchen.

"Sure," she said.

We gave Squirt his juice. The chaos and noise continued around us.

And then Squirt, well, gave me the juice.

"Oops," I said. "His diaper needs changing."

I stood up.

"You're it," said David Michael, whizzing by me and tagging Margo. "You're the turkey."

"Don't run in the house," I said automatically.

"It's okay," said Margo. "We're playing Pilgrims chasing the turkey."

If I were a turkey, I thought, I'd *hate* Thanksgiving.

"Okay, Squirt," I said. Over my shoulder I said, "I'm going to change Squirt."

I heard a chair turn over in the Pikes' family room.

"Uh-oh," I said, heading toward the sound.

Just then Dawn walked through the door.

"Here," I said. "Can you take Squirt? He needs changing and I . . . I . . . I . . ." My voice trailed off.

Then I shrieked so loudly that you could have heard me in the next state. "DAWN, DAWN, IT'S DAWN!"

I flung myself at her, just managing to remember not to squash Squirt between us.

As we hugged, I heard Mary Anne's gasp. "It *is* you. Oh, Dawn."

Well, from there we went into a BSC huddle, all hugging each other, and Dawn, and exclaiming, "I don't believe it!" and "How did you get here?"

When Dawn broke free of the huddle, she turned to find herself face-to-face with Abby. "You're not Dawn Schafer, are you?" asked Abby with a perfectly straight face.

We started laughing and talking all over again, introducing Dawn and Abby, and trying to tell Dawn everything that had happened since we'd last seen her. As we talked, we surged back into the kitchen, and Dawn grabbed a chair at the kitchen table.

That's when I realized that I was still holding Squirt, who was taking things very calmly, and that a chair was still tipped over in the other room. Turning Squirt wet side out, I found the chair, righted it, and returned to the kitchen to find Dawn examining a cookie with cranberry eyes. "Very nice, Claire," she said. "Thank you. I'm going to save it."

"Can I have the eyes, then?" asked Claire.

Laughing, Dawn gave Claire the two cranberry eyes.

I couldn't believe my own eyes. It really was Dawn — tanned, with her long, pale blonde hair and friendly blue eyes, looking as relaxed and at home and, well, as Dawn-like as ever. I had wondered what would happen when Dawn and Abby finally met, since they were so very, very different. But they were totally cool, as if they had been BSC members together.

We were all extremely excited. Mary Anne, naturally, was a little misty-eyed, too, as Dawn told us how much she'd missed us. "So I decided to come to Stoneybrook for Thanksgiving. Then I decided I wanted it to be a surprise. Everyone helped me keep it a secret, and here I am."

"I don't believe it, I just don't believe it," said Mary Anne. "I am so, so glad you are here."

"Me, too, and that's true," said Vanessa. "Want to see my place mats, Dawn?"

"Come play with us," urged Adam.

"I better go change Squirt," I said.

"Hey, I can handle that," said Dawn with a grin, standing up. She took Squirt. "You are so cute." She wrinkled her nose. "And so wet."

Holding Squirt, who had grabbed a fistful of Dawn's hair, she left the kitchen.

Mary Anne dabbed at her eyes.

Then Kristy clapped her hand to her forehead in mock dismay. "Dinner for thirty-*seven*! What are we going to do?" she cried.

CHAPTER 15

It was a cold and gloomy day, a pre-snow brooding gray.

But who cared? It was Thanksgiving. No school for four whole days. And a Thanksgiving feast of turkey and crane berries (the Pilgrims really did call them that because of the shape of the branches of the cranberry bushes) and a whole lot more of my favorite foods, both traditional and nontraditional. No oysters, though.

I mentioned this to Janine as we rode to Kristy's house at noon.

"How can people eat oysters raw?" I asked. "It's enough to make you a vegetarian or something."

"Some vegetarians say that their rule is never to eat anything that has a face," said Janine. She paused. "Do oysters have faces?"

"Good one, Janine," I said. "You should ask

Dawn. It sounds like her kind of question to me."

Janine allowed herself a small smile. "Maybe I will," she said.

When we reached Kristy's, we unloaded a card table, extra chairs, napkins, and a pumpkin pie that my mom and dad had made the night before, after Mom had come home from work. (My dad had left work early and gone over to the Brewer-Thomases to help with the cooking and cleaning the day before.)

Stacey and her mother were wrestling chairs through the front door, dodging Nannie, who was fastening a Thanksgiving display of multicolored corn to the front door.

I carried the pumpkin pie into the kitchen.

The kitchen was awesome. The smell of roasting turkey filled the air. I bent over and peered through the oven window at the massive bird. But I couldn't help worrying that it wouldn't be big enough.

"Don't worry," Kristy assured me, when I asked her about this. "The Pikes are bringing another ten-ton turkey, too."

"You sounded like Vanessa, on her way to a rhyme," Mal's voice said at that minute. We turned to see her step aside. Mr. Pike came into the kitchen, holding an enormous roasting pan with a huge tinfoil hump in the middle.

Watson cried, "Over here, over here," pointing to the only clear spot on the butcher-block counter.

Every available surface was covered: I could see pecan, pumpkin, and apple-cranberry pies, cranberry sauce, and a sweet potato casserole with little marshmallows on top. Plain potatoes were boiling on the stove to be made into mashed potatoes at the last minute. I saw string beans and carrots. Rolls stood on trays ready to be put into the oven. Kristy's mother was making gravy.

Dawn and Mary Anne arrived carrying a huge pot. "Pumpkin soup," Dawn announced. "It's very good for you. It's sweet, too, but that's its natural flavor. No added sugar."

I hid a smile. Dawn might have moved back to California, but she hadn't changed.

I left them to help with the card tables in the library and den.

Abby, Anna, and Janine had begun setting the tables, with a little help from Claire.

"You turn the knife blade toward the plate, Claire," I heard Janine explain.

"Why?" asked Claire.

Abby and Anna looked up. I waited.

"Because," said Janine at last. "That's why."

I couldn't help it. I started laughing.

Nannie and David Michael had made centerpieces for the tables, and I had written name cards in careful calligraphy for each place. We hadn't wanted a roomful of kids eating Thanksgiving dinner completely unsupervised. After all, the kids in our play had managed to start a sword fight with cardboard turkey legs. There was some argument about who was going to sit where, but everything turned out okay.

Mr. Ramsey had brought his video camera. When the tables were set, he went from room to room filming them. We'd put gaily patterned tablecloths on the tables, and the place mats Vanessa and Sam had made were bright splashes of color at each chair.

In the dining room, I could hear our parents talking and laughing as they added leaves to the big formal table and spread a snowy white tablecloth across it. Watson took silver from a sideboard and gave it to Dawn's mother, who began setting the places.

"Uh, the, um, knives face in toward the plate," I heard Watson say.

Although thirty-seven people including twenty-three kids were there, everyone was on their best behavior. For the kids, it meant trying hard to keep their excitement under control. We burned off some of their energy putting up the decorations we'd made during our marathon baby-sitting job the day before.

At two o'clock, we sat down to Thanksgiving dinner.

What can I say? Most of my favorite people, and most of my favorite foods, were gathered together under one roof. We set up the food buffet style, and let everyone serve themselves — although some of the younger kids needed a little help. I was practically staggering under the weight of my plate as I went to my seat, at a card table in the library. Stacey waved to me from another card table.

I looked around at my dining companions: Margo, David Michael, and Sam. "Hi," I said. "Happy Thanksgiving, guys."

It was a feast of noble proportions. (That was a line from both versions of the Thanksgiving play.) We ate and ate, and talked and talked. Then we took a break from eating so we would have room for dessert.

We sang Thanksgiving songs and Christmas songs and silly songs.

I ate three kinds of pie and ice cream. I would have eaten more, if my stomach had had the noble proportions to match the feast. But I still managed to do quite a bit of picking and snacking during our cleanup.

By late afternoon, we were all moving in super-slow motion, even Dawn, who was still on West Coast time, which meant it felt three

127

hours earlier to her. Everyone began to get ready to go home.

The day had gone so fast! I didn't want it to end.

Suddenly I heard Vanessa shout, "Oh, oh, oh, it's *snoooow!*"

We hurried to the door. Fat white flakes of snow were twirling gently down through the darkening air. No matter how many times I see snow, it always amazes me. I put my arms out and let the flakes tickle them.

Then I shivered. "It's cold," I said.

We loaded up the car. I turned to look at the others — Kristy's family gathered in the doorway, waving; the Pikes, bursting out of the Pikemobile; Dawn and Mary Anne sitting happily next to one another in their backseat; Abby and Anna and their mother heading for the sidewalk that led toward their house; Stacey and her mom getting into their car; Jessi rocking Squirt gently in her arms as she talked to Mal, who was about to join her family.

I was suddenly so happy that I couldn't stand it, so happy I thought I would burst. I rolled down the window. Leaning as far out as I could, I shouted, for all my friends and all the world to hear: *"Happy Thanksgiving, everyone! Happy Thanksgiving!"*

What else could I say about the best Thanksgiving ever?

Dear Reader,

Claudia and the First Thanksgiving is one of the first
holiday stories in the Baby-sitters Club series. Like
Kristy's little sister Karen, I love holidays. And I
especially like a large gathering of people for
Thanksgiving dinner, although I never attended
Thanksgiving for 37 people!

Like Claudia in this book, I think that no matter
what the background of Thanksgiving, it is a
wonderful holiday — a time to celebrate with family
and friends, and to be thankful for what we have.
Over the years I've celebrated the holiday in many
different cities and many different settings. I don't
remember every single Thanksgiving, but the most
memorable one when I was growing up was the year
the oven caught fire, and the firefighters had to come
over to put out the fire before we could eat!

Happy reading,

Ann M. Martin

L. GODWIN

Ann M. Martin

About the Author

ANN MATTHEWS MARTIN was born on August 12, 1955. She grew up in Princeton, NJ, with her parents and her younger sister, Jane.

Although Ann used to be a teacher and then an editor of children's books, she's now a full-time writer. She gets the ideas for her books from many different places. Some are based on personal experiences. Others are based on childhood memories and feelings. Many are written about contemporary problems or events.

All of Ann's characters, even the members of the Baby-sitters Club, are made up. (So is Stoneybrook.) But many of her characters are based on real people. Sometimes Ann names her characters after people she knows, other times she chooses names she likes.

In addition to the Baby-sitters Club books, Ann Martin has written many other books for children. Her favorite is *Ten Kids, No Pets* because she loves big families and she loves animals. Her favorite Baby-sitters Club book is *Kristy's Big Day*. (By the way, Kristy is her favorite baby-sitter!)

Ann M. Martin now lives in New York. She has two cats, Mouse and Rosie (who's a boy, but that's a long story). Her hobbies are reading, sewing, and needlework — especially making clothes for children.

Notebook Pages

This Baby-sitters Club book belongs to _____.

I am _____ years old and in the _____ grade.

The name of my school is _____.

I got this BSC book from _____.

I started reading it on _____ and

finished reading it on _____.

The place where I read most of this book is _____.

My favorite part was when _____.

If I could change anything in the story, it might be the part when

_____.

My favorite character in the Baby-sitters Club is _____.

The BSC member I am most like is _____

because _____.

If I could write a Baby-sitters Club book it would be about ___

_____

_____.

#91 Claudia and the First Thanksgiving

Claudia and the other BSC members have to plan a Thanksgiving dinner for 37 people. The most people I've ever had Thanksgiving dinner with is _____. The place I usually go for Thanksgiving is _____. It takes me _____ hours to get there. The farthest I've ever gone for Thanksgiving dinner was when _____. The funniest thing that's ever happened to me on Thanksgiving was when _____ _____.

If I were hosting Thanksgiving dinner I would be sure to invite _____. We would eat _____, and for decorations, I would _____. My favorite Thanksgiving food is _____. My least favorite Thanksgiving food is _____. Claudia and her Short Takes class put on a play about the Thanksgiving story. If I were writing a play with my class, I would want it to be about _____ _____. For Claudia's play, Betsy Sobak is given the starring role. In my play, I would want _____ to be the star. I would give myself the role of _____ _____.

CLAUDIA'S

Finger painting at 3...

A spooky sitting adventure

Sitting for two of my favorite charges --
Jamie and Lucy Newton.

SCRAPBOOK

...oil painting
at 13!

my family. Mom and Dad, me and
Janine... and we'll never forget mimi.

Read all the books
about **Claudia**
in the Baby-sitters Club series
by Ann M. Martin

Look for #92

MALLORY'S CHRISTMAS WISH

"On the first day of Christmas . . ." our voices began.

Ding-dong!

"I'll get it!" three or four of my siblings shouted.

Mom shut the recorder. "I knew it. It's the Christmas Carol Police, coming to arrest us."

A man stood on the porch.

"Mrs. Pike?" he said.

"Yes," my mom answered.

"My name is Chad Henry. I'm a producer/director for Channel Three TV, and I wanted to congratulate you in person. You've been selected out of hundreds of contestants —"

Vanessa came running to the door. She looked about ready to lift off the ground. "The Old-fashioned Christmas Contest?" she blurted out.

"That's right," Mr. Henry said. "Are you Vanessa?"

Vanessa shrieked and began hopping around the living room.

Eight baffled pairs of eyes watched her, then turned back to Mr. Henry.

"What is this all about?" Mom asked.

"Didn't you see the commercial?" Vanessa cried. "All you had to do was write a letter about the way your family was going to spend Christmas. And Mallory was saying how we had to have this old-style Christmas and all, so I entered us. I figured we'd be perfect."

"Your entry was sensational, Vanessa," Mr. Henry said. "I have to compliment you, Mrs. Pike. What a family. Eight children — and yet such a strong sense of closeness and traditional American values. Warmth, generosity, wholesomeness . . ."

As Mr. Henry searched for another word, Mom said, "What exactly does this contest entail? Do we have to buy anything?"

Mr. Henry chuckled and reached into his jacket pocket. "On the contrary, Mrs. Pike,."

We all gathered around as Mr. Henry pulled out an envelope and removed a check from it.

I thought my jaw was going to hit the floor as I read it.

"Ten thousand dollars?" my mom said.

by Ann M. Martin

More titles... ▶

❑ MG47011-6	#73 Mary Anne and Miss Priss	$3.50
❑ MG47012-4	#74 Kristy and the Copycat	$3.50
❑ MG47013-2	#75 Jessi's Horrible Prank	$3.50
❑ MG47014-0	#76 Stacey's Lie	$3.50
❑ MG48221-1	#77 Dawn and Whitney, Friends Forever	$3.50
❑ MG48222-X	#78 Claudia and Crazy Peaches	$3.50
❑ MG48223-8	#79 Mary Anne Breaks the Rules	$3.50
❑ MG48224-6	#80 Mallory Pike, #1 Fan	$3.50
❑ MG48225-4	#81 Kristy and Mr. Mom	$3.50
❑ MG48226-2	#82 Jessi and the Troublemaker	$3.50
❑ MG48235-1	#83 Stacey vs. the BSC	$3.50
❑ MG48228-9	#84 Dawn and the School Spirit War	$3.50
❑ MG48236-X	#85 Claudi Kishi, Live from WSTO	$3.50
❑ MG48227-0	#86 Mary Anne and Camp BSC	$3.50
❑ MG48237-8	#87 Stacey and the Bad Girls	$3.50
❑ MG22872-2	#88 Farewell, Dawn	$3.50
❑ MG22873-0	#89 Kristy and the Dirty Diapers	$3.50
❑ MG45575-3	Logan's Story Special Edition Readers' Request	$3.25
❑ MG47110-X	Logan Bruno, Boy Baby-sitter Special Edition Readers' Request	$3.50
❑ MG47756-0	Shannon's Story Special Edition	$3.50
❑ MG44240-6	Baby-sitters on Board! Super Special #1	$3.95
❑ MG44239-2	Baby-sitters' Summer Vacation Super Special #2	$3.95
❑ MG43973-1	Baby-sitters' Winter Vacation Super Special #3	$3.95
❑ MG42493-9	Baby-sitters' Island Adventure Super Special #4	$3.95
❑ MG43575-2	California Girls! Super Special #5	$3.95
❑ MG43576-0	New York, New York! Super Special #6	$3.95
❑ MG44963-X	Snowbound Super Special #7	$3.95
❑ MG44962-X	Baby-sitters at Shadow Lake Super Special #8	$3.95
❑ MG45661-X	Starring the Baby-sitters Club Super Special #9	$3.95
❑ MG45674-1	Sea City, Here We Come! Super Special #10	$3.95
❑ MG47015-9	The Baby-sitter's Remember Super Special #11	$3.95
❑ MG48308-0	Here Come the Bridesmaids Super Special #12	$3.95

Available wherever you buy books...or use this order form.

Scholastic Inc., P.O. Box 7502, 2931 E. McCarty Street, Jefferson City, MO 65102

Please send me the books I have checked above. I am enclosing $ _____ (please add $2.00 to cover shipping and handling). Send check or money order—no cash or C.O.D.s please.

Name _____ Birthdate _____

Address _____

City _____ State/Zip _____

Please allow four to six weeks for delivery. Offer good in the U.S. only. Sorry, mail orders are not available to residents of Canada. Prices subject to change.

THE BABY-SITTERS CLUB®

ALL NEW!

by Ann M. Martin

Meet the best friends you'll ever have!

Have you heard? The BSC has a new look—and more great stuff than ever before. An all-new scrapbook for each book's narrator! A letter from Ann M. Martin! Fill-in pages to personalize your copy! Order today!

❑ BBD22473-5	#1	Kristy's Great Idea	$3.50
❑ BBD22763-7	#2	Claudia and the Phantom Phone Calls	$3.50
❑ BBD25158-9	#3	The Truth About Stacey	$3.50
❑ BBD25159-7	#4	Mary Anne Saves the Day	$3.50
❑ BBD25160-0	#5	Dawn and the Impossible Three	$3.50

Available wherever you buy books, or use this order form.

Send orders to Scholastic Inc., P.O. Box 7500, 2931 East McCarty Street, Jefferson City, MO 65102.

Please send me the books I have checked above. I am enclosing $_____ (please add $2.00 to cover shipping and handling). Send check or money order—no cash or C.O.D.s please.

Please allow four to six weeks for delivery. Offer good in the U.S.A. only. Sorry, mail orders are not available to residents in Canada. Prices subject to change.

Name_____Birthdate ___/___/___
      First   Last   D / M / Y
Address_____
City_____ State_____ Zip_____
Telephone ( ) _____ ❑ Boy   ❑ Girl

Where did you buy this book? Bookstore ❑   Book Fair ❑
                                   Book Club ❑   Other ❑

■ SCHOLASTIC

BSCE395

Now THE BABY-SITTERS CLUB®

★ is a Video Club too! ★

What's the scoop with Dawn, Kristy, Mallory, and the other girls?

Be the first to know with G★I★R★L★ magazine!

Hey, Baby-sitters Club readers! Now you can be the first on the block to get in on the action of G★I★R★L★ It's an exciting new magazine that lets you dig in and read...

★ Upcoming selections from Ann Martin's Baby-sitters Club books
★ Fun articles on handling stress, turning dreams into great careers, making and keeping best friends, and much more
★ Plus, all the latest on new movies, books, music, and sports!

To get in on the scoop, just cut and mail this coupon today. And don't forget to tell all your friends about G★I★R★L★ magazine!

A neat offer for you...6 issues for only $15.00.

Sign up today -- this special offer ends July 1, 1996!

❑ **YES!** Please send me G★I★R★L★ magazine. I will receive six fun-filled issues for only $15.00. Enclosed is a check (no cash, please) made payable to G★I★R★L★ for $15.00.

Just fill in, cut out, and mail this coupon with your payment of $15.00 to:
G★I★R★L★, c/o Scholastic Inc., 2931 East McCarty Street, Jefferson City, MO 65101.

Name _____

Address _____

City, State, ZIP _____

9013